Obituary Column

Sandra Farris and Dan Farris

iUniverse, Inc.
New York Bloomington

Obituary Column

iUniverse books may be ordered through booksellers or by contacting:

iUniverse
1663 Liberty Drive
Bloomington, IN 47403
www.iuniverse.com
1-800-Authors (1-800-288-4677)

ISBN: 978-1-4401-6052-3 (sc)
ISBN: 978-1-4401-6050-9 (dj)
ISBN: 978-1-4401-6051-6 (ebk)

Printed in the United States of America

iUniverse rev. date: 8/21/2009

Other Books by Sandra Farris

Wind Dancers (Co-Author, Darlene McKeen)

Can You Hear the Music?

Lady Ace

Acknowledgement

Cover by Dennis Farris

This book is dedicated with love to my family and friends, with special thanks to Melinda Islas for her help. Also to Trystan Lomen and Virginia "Sally" Ellis.

Sandra Farris

Forget Me Not

Forget me not, forget me never
When yonder sun shall set forever
Hills and mountains divide us
You, I cannot see,
Just take pen and paper and write to me.
Blue waters may be between us roll
And distance be our lot
But if we fail to meet again,
Dearest loved one, forget me not.

M.G. Owens
April 16, 1948

This poem is one of many written by my great-grandfather in letters to my mother, but it is the only one our family has now.

A Love Remembered

It seems like an eternity
Since we said goodbye.
Softly you turned and kissed me
And disappeared into the night.
I've missed you so much thru the years
You were my life, my love, my all.
My heart still aches 'cause you're not here
But my future began to call.
I close my eyes and reminisce
Of early days of you and me
Those glory days, then I wish
For one more day spent quietly
To hear your voice and feel your touch
To see your eyes that smile
How I miss you dear so much
But if I listen for a while
I hear your voice in the night
When things are dark and still
You call to me of sweeter times
Of climbing trees and hills
My life with you was innocent
And I never felt regret
It was a time of love well spent
And tho you're gone, I will never forget.

Darlene McKeen

This poem was written by my sister, great granddaughter of M.G. Owens.

Sandra Farris

Prologue

Berlin, Germany, 1938

"Papa, can't you please come with us?" Hannah Levine pleaded.

"I have some things— " Samuel began, but Esther put her fingers against his lips and glanced around. "— to do first," he finished, speaking around her fingers. He frowned and then nodded to his wife. He knew to be careful with his words without any warning from her. "You go with your mother, Hannah, and mind what she tells you. Promise me."

"I will, I promise." Tears welled in her eyes as she clutched her father's hand. In her eight years Hannah had never been away from her father for more than a day. Now, she was not sure when she would see him again.

Samuel knelt down, pulled her coat more tightly around her, fastening the top buttons, and then he tucked her knitted scarf into the neckline so no cold could get in. He wiped the tears from her cheeks and kissed her gently, while he mentally recorded this moment. Another time and another place he could withdraw the memory to help him through the difficult times he knew were ahead.

Steam hissed white vapors into the cold November night and a sharp whistle announced the imminent departure of the train. Samuel glanced at the few travelers and people bidding them farewell. Only a couple of soldiers walked along the platform, but he knew that would soon change. Already there were unannounced "inspections" of businesses and seizures of the owners' valuables. Samuel knew it was only a matter of time before an exodus began, and the departures would be scrutinized more closely.

One soldier looked their way and then said something to his comrade. They started walking toward Samuel, but were stopped by a white haired man and his wife. Hesitantly, they listened to the older couple but continued to look at Samuel.

"All aboard," called the conductor.

"What about— you-know-who?" Esther asked, a hint of panic in her voice. She was too frightened even to speak his name.

"Don't worry Esther. I have that taken care of. Hurry now," he urged, ushering his wife on board.

"When will you join us, Samuel?" Esther tearfully asked from the steps of the train. She braced herself against the doorway as the train lurched forward.

"Soon— as soon as I can. Take care Esther, and always be alert."

The train began to move and Samuel walked back into the station. He pulled his collar up against the cold and pushed through the station's front doors, into the night. His stride was purposeful, but not so much as to raise alarm, as he walked toward the waiting taxicab. Seated inside, Samuel leaned forward and gave the driver an address. When he glanced back at the station through the steam-covered window, he saw the two Gestapo soldiers burst through the door. This time he was ahead of them. Next time . . .

Chapter One

Monet Cove, California, Present Day

Tracy Chapman ran a tapered nail down the newspaper column until an item caught her interest. She folded the page in half and read it carefully.

Samuel Levine, born in Berlin, Germany, September 23,1912.

The microwave beeped and she hesitantly pulled her attention from the paper. She had a desperate need for that cup of coffee right now. The giant margarita, sipped before dinner, left her with a terrible headache this morning. The frothy liquid had tasted so good last night, too.

"Stay where you are, I'll get that for you."

She patted the strong hand on her shoulder and returned her gaze to the newspaper. "Could you hand me the phone, too, Michael? You're such a dear. I could easily let you spoil me rotten."

After handing her the phone, Michael heaped a spoonful of instant coffee into the cup of hot water, adding a splash of milk. He stirred the mixture and brought it to the table.

"Doing your ghoul job already?" Michael asked, glancing over her shoulder.

Tracy picked up the newspaper and swatted at him. "Michael Harris, don't tell me you don't read the obituary column? Millions of people read them."

"Sure I do," he said and grinned. "Occasionally." His powerful body moved with an easy grace as he walked around the table and eased into the chair opposite Tracy. "You don't think I want to be left out of numbers like that." He tilted his head to one side. "Do that many people really read the obits?"

"I don't know, but a lot of people read them." She glanced up. "You're never intrigued when you don't see a family listed? Don't you ever wonder about these people?"

"What do you mean?"

"Well, like what kind of life did they have? Did they ever fulfill their dreams? What about their family? "

"No, not really— well, maybe a little since you do what you do."

Tracy dialed Herb Johnston, the local Medical Examiner. She worked with him and the police often, locating families of the deceased, unless the death involved a criminal matter. With all the budget cuts the last few years, there was a manpower shortage in many of Monet Cove's government offices.

"Hi, Tracy. I was just going to call you. I took the liberty of giving your name and phone number to Mrs. Bidwell. She's the woman who owns the apartment building where Mr. Levine lived. I told her to give you a call." He shuffled through papers and continued, "We got in touch with the German Embassy in L.A. day before yesterday when they brought Mr. Levine in. Even though he lived here for many years, we thought they might check in Germany for relatives. They were going to run an ad in the newspapers; probably ran yesterday because they said they would get right on it."

"Thanks, Herb. I'll wait to hear from her. Meanwhile, if you hear anything from Germany let me know."

"Hopefully, we can find the family very soon. Jewish faith dictates that the body is buried right away. However, there are special circumstances, this of course, being one of them."

"I'll certainly do my best. Keep in touch and I'll let you know about my progress." Then to Michael, "It won't take me long to shower and get ready. "Make sure you packed everything and I'll be with you in a moment." She tore out the column before tossing the paper into the recycle bin.

"If there is a family somewhere, certainly they would want to be informed as soon as possible. I just can't believe he has no one; that there is no one left in this world who cared for him." Her thoughts went to her brother. Although he had disappeared twenty-two years earlier, when she lifted her amber eyes pain still flickered there.

Tracy was twenty when her sixteen-year old brother, Chase, went missing. It took five years for her family to find out he had been murdered in Florida. Chase had no identification on him when the authorities found his body, and they had no missing person report that matched his description. After a time they finally buried him as a "John Doe".

Tracy was the one who searched for her brother. The process almost defeated her, but she refused to give in. Her persistence paid off seventeen years ago and she remembered that day well—

* * * * * * * * *

Large raindrops pelted her bright red umbrella in a rat-a-tat staccato, while thunder rolled in from the sea and across the sky. Tracy ran from her rented car to the grey stone building housing the police department. She dodged puddles forming on the pavement as she hurried down the walkway. Wiping her feet on the doormat, Tracy closed her umbrella just inside the door.

"Miss Chapman?"

"Yes, I'm Tracy Chapman— Officer Burke?"

"Looks like you got here just in time." He nodded toward the storm outside.

"Is this going to be one of your infamous hurricanes?"

"No, at least according to the weather forecasts." Officer Burke punched in a few numbers on the door lock and opened it, allowing Tracy to enter. "Go down this hall and the second door on your right is my office. Have a seat and I'll be there in a minute. Would you like something to drink?"

"A stiff shot of whiskey would be good right now." She offered a nervous smile, though more like a twitch, and added, "But a cup of coffee will be fine." Butterflies fluttered wildly in her stomach. The inside of her mouth was suddenly very dry.

The search was finally over after five long years. As discouraging as it had been, she still held out hope this wouldn't be Chase, that he was still somewhere out there alive.

Burke stuck his head through the doorway, "Cream and sugar?"

"Cream only, please."

"I'll be right back."

Tracy left her chair and looked out the window. Rain was coming down steadily, obscuring the view. Trees and buildings were shaded in somber grey silhouettes. The weather matched her emotions well.

When Officer Burke returned, he stood a few feet behind Tracy for a minute, not wanting to intrude upon her quiet introspective. She sensed his presence and turned from the window, grief drawing lines upon her face. He handed her the coffee and went behind his desk. Removing a file folder from under his arm, Burke opened it and retrieved a photograph. He looked at it for a minute as though deciding whether to show it.

Suddenly Tracy became aware her nails were digging into her palms. She tried to relax but ended up gripping the arm of the chair tightly, her knuckles white-capped.

"Are you sure you're ready for this?"

"I've been ready for five years, Officer. I'm just— "

"I understand."

He passed the photograph across his desk. Tracy stared at the white piece of paper for a minute. Her hand trembled when she finally reached for it and she drew a deep breath before righting the picture. Her brother's pale face filled the square. Chase's eyes, shades of amber and green, the same color as her own, were closed in death's slumber. His hair matched hers too, except in summer the sun painted golden highlights in his, while hers remained a light brown.

His face, alive and handsome, flashed in her mind. A mouth, always curled as if on the edge of laughter, was now only a slash below his nose; a nose she rarely saw without the white coating surfers used to prevent sunburn.

Her moan filled the room and Tracy was engulfed in a black wave of unconsciousness.

The trip to the cemetery the next day was harder yet. At least the weather was picture perfect. Blue skies met blue ocean with only a wispy cloud or two floating lazily overhead. A soft sea breeze stirred palm fronds and shrubs at the entrance to Green Meadows Cemetery and Mortuary.

The paved drive through the cemetery was immaculate. A green carpet of grass undulated above the rise and fall of the grounds, while trees provided cool shade for the occasional visitor.

The officer followed the winding drive and stopped at the back of the cemetery. He hurried around to her side of the car and opened the door. Glancing up from the piece of paper in his hand, he surveyed the landscape.

Tracy picked up the bouquet of white carnations, roses and baby's breath she had bought earlier and slowly emerged from the car. She stood a moment, her gaze sweeping the area, as she fought to keep her fragile control.

"I think it's right over here." He climbed the slope and stopped at the third row of plaques. "Yes, here it is. I'll leave you alone and you just let me know when you're ready to leave."

"Thank you, Officer Murphy." Her voice was barely above a whisper. Before looking down at the grave, she glanced out across the cemetery. White-caps peaked on the ocean waves, indicating a new storm forming in the distance. Soon the waves would climb high and crash, turning to foam and rushing ashore. Tiny sailboats raced toward marinas, the boats appearing larger as they came nearer the shore. Sea gulls called to one another as they flew the coastline, some drifting inland. It was a beautiful scene for an eternal resting place and how fitting for an avid surfer.

Tears trembled beneath her eyelids, and her clamped lips imprisoned a sob. Slowly, she knelt and placed the flowers on the grave. Her hand caressed the sign, "John Doe, No. 3". Then she wept aloud, rocking back and forth . . .

* * * * * * * * *

Tracy never forgot the agony she and her family suffered those five years not knowing where her brother was. Just as painful was the heartbreak of his dying alone. Had he been frightened, knowing his fate, or had it been quick and unexpected— the gunshot that had ended his life? She hoped the latter was true, that there had been no time for fear.

The difficulty of searching for and finding her brother didn't begin to compare with the job of telling her mother. Afterward, so consumed with grief, Rose Chapman moved to Florida to be close to Chase, shutting out the rest of her family. Her marriage became a casualty of that sorrow, which also caused the estrangement between mother and daughter. Rose never fully recovered from the tragedy and, as far as Tracy knew, was still in Florida.

Her father chose to run from his grief, traveling the world until his death three years ago. She always thought the grief finally caught up with him and his heart broke irreparably.

It was Tracy's search that sparked an interest in locating missing families of the deceased, hoping to spare them the same extended grief. With the age of computers and twenty some years of research under her belt, she had considerably narrowed down the time it took to locate families.

Tracy's main job was her antique shop, Another Tyme, over which she lived. It was filled with items given to her by grateful families, or bought at estate sales. Her business did well enough that she hired Amy Bryant to manage it. The antique shop also allowed her the time and funds to pursue the more fulfilling purpose in her life. It was a sad day when she failed in her mission, the results of which were burials in a "potter's field". Fortunately, those were few.

"Then you are going to make an honest man out of me?" Amusement flickered in the eyes that met hers. "Let me spoil you rotten?"

Tracy gave him a blank look.

"You were saying before the phone call." Michael watched several different emotions play across her face.

"Oh, yes, I remember. Now why would I go and do something like that? It's much more interesting this way, don't you think?" Tracy answered lightly, but she looked deep into his eyes to see if he really was serious. During the three years of their relationship, the conversation had come up before and both agreed they were not ready for that kind of commitment again. Besides, things were just fine as they were.

"Are you going to take me to the airport?" Michael changed the subject. He glanced at his watch— seven A.M "I have a ten-thirty flight you know."

Michael seemed edgy this morning, or maybe it was just her imagination. Tracy gave his expression a closer examination. His dark brown hair, still damp from his shower, looked black, making the silver streaks at his temples gleam brighter. Her gaze moved down to his handsome face, bronzed by continued exposure to the wind and sun. A muscle clenched along his jaw, then eased as he gave her one of his intriguing smiles. Feather-like laugh lines crinkled around his Nordic blue eyes, a feature that had captured Tracy's heart.

"Are you all right?" She asked.

"Me? Sure. Why do you ask?"

"You just seem—never mind. Thanks for the coffee. It won't take me long. Make sure you packed everything and I'll be with you in a moment," she repeated her earlier statement.

"I'll double check. Need any help?"

"If you want to get to the airport on time, you'd better just stick with the double checking." Tracy grinned seductively. Tiptoeing, she placed a light kiss on his mouth. "Be right out."

Michael moved to the counter and rinsed out his cup, putting it in the dishwasher. He looked around the galley kitchen making sure everything was in order before he went through the living room and out onto the deck. Squinting against the bright morning sunlight, he leaned his forearms on the railing and watched the waves crest and race ashore. Frothy foam was the beach before it was dragged back out to sea, only to repeat the process. There was something very calming about the movement of all that water. This morning he needed that calming effect. At the moment the reason escaped him.

Brightly colored sailboats dotted the ocean, taking advantage of the breeze. In the background a large container ship skulked across the horizon and beyond that the azure sky dipped into the sea at what seemed the very edge of the earth. One could understand why, at one time, early man thought they would fall off if they ventured too far.

"Rutger Dietrick?" The voice on the other end of the phone spoke in German.

"Who is this?" Dietrick countered, his English hampered by a strong German accent. "What's your business?"

"I am calling on behalf of a friend of yours. He said there was something in the paper today that would be of great interest to you."

"I'm listening."

"A fellow countryman passed in the United States and they are trying to notify the family."

"His name?" Dietrick prompted impatiently.

"Samuel Levine, born 1912 in Germany. He has been a resident of Monet Cove, California for the past 18 years." The voice hesitated. "Could be you are interested in this Samuel Levine?"

"Tell my friend I appreciate his thoughtfulness and that I will be in touch with him once I get to California. I would like him to fax me a copy of that article at once."

Dietrick disconnected the call and dialed the local airport. "I need a flight to— " he glanced at his scribbling, "— Monet Cove, California, as soon as possible. You don't fly there? How close do you go? San Jose will be fine. In an hour and a half? How long is the flight? Two hours. Excellent. I will also need the use of an automobile. Das goot—good." He hung up the phone, gripping it tightly and said, "Well, Herr Levine, it appears I win after all. I will get back what's mine and no one will stand in my way this time."

Chapter Two

"Now, Cowboy, are you ready to go?" Tracy walked out onto the deck behind Michael and slid her arms around his middle. She leaned her head against his back. "Mm-m-m, you smell good. Sure you don't want to stay a little longer?"

Michael turned and faced her. A melancholy frown flitted across his features. "I've been away from the ranch too long as it is. Come with me, Tracy."

"You know I can't do that right now. I have to train hard for my kickboxing tournament. Even though it's almost three weeks away, I won't have a lot of time, what with this new assignment and all." She studied his face again. "What's up? You've been— well, different this morning. Something going on you're not telling me?"

"No," he answered. For an instant, wistfulness crept into his expression, but he switched it off just as quickly. He turned and went back inside and Tracy joined him. "We'd better get a move on or I'll miss my plane. When *do* you think you'll be coming out to North Dakota? It's your turn, you know. I've been here twice in a row now." He tried to make his question light-hearted, but somehow it just didn't come out that way. He was serious, even though he knew what her answer would be. It was always so hard to leave her. Lately it seemed even more difficult.

They hardly spent time together any more when he was here with her; she was usually occupied with work or kickboxing and that had Michael worried. He was afraid the quality of their relationship was beginning to suffer. Now wasn't the time to bring it up, though. He didn't want to leave her with a possible argument hanging between them.

When Tracy shrugged her shoulders in answer to his question, Michael kissed her on the forehead. He picked up his bags and strode toward the door. Tracy followed, turning to lock up behind her.

Monet Cove lay between sprawling Los Angeles to the south and San Francisco to the north. The location, with its natural beauty, quaint shops and restaurants, attracted visitors from both metropolitan areas. At one end of town, a small cove with rocky cliffs above the Pacific Ocean drew a large number of bird watchers as well.

It began as a gathering place for artists in the mid 1800's, around the time of the impressionist movement in Europe. Some American artists aspired to be like their counterparts overseas and the natural beauty of the area lent itself well to their aspirations. To this day nearby meadows with their wildflowers still lure landscape artists with varying degrees of talent.

Tracy drove in silence for a time, enjoying the scenery along the coast before she turned inland toward San Jose. Michael, too, watched the countryside slip by. He seemed pensive, not disturbed or angry. His thoughts were on the ninety-minute trip ahead and saying goodbye to Tracy. He didn't know when he would see her again. The ranch was taking more of his time and Tracy seemed pretty much involved with this new case. Who knew how long that would take? He tried to keep from pressuring her about their relationship, because in the beginning they agreed the best thing for them both was to live separately.

Three years earlier, they had been seated next to each other on an airplane headed to San Francisco from connecting flights in Denver. He was going to San Francisco for a business meeting, she was returning from an antique buying trip with a detour to San Francisco instead of her usual destination of San Jose. Exchanging information, they kept in touch via correspondence, then phone calls, followed by alternating visits with each other. One thing led to another and they fell in love.

Tracy had never married in her forty-two years. She had come close a couple of times but both experiences had been disastrous. The second relationship with Mark Horner, had been the worst. Mark dominated everything in his life, including his women. Under his control almost a year, Tracy finally came to her senses and broke it off. The break did not come easily, however, and she vowed not to fall into that trap again. She wanted never to sacrifice her liberties a second time. Freedom meant too much to her; Michael felt the same way.

Michael had married his high school sweetheart right after college, a union he lived to regret. His life, too, had not been his own and the result was a constant verbal war. When the marriage was over it cost him a great deal of money and he almost lost the ranch, which had been in his family for generations.

Tracy glanced sideways at Michael. He seemed to have retreated into a world of his own and she broke the spell, "You haven't talked much about the ranch."

"It's keeping me busy," Michael shrugged matter-of-factly, "and I was just thinking that I wasn't sure when I could get back this way."

"Maybe I can get my business over with soon. I'd like to visit your place again and go horseback riding with you and— Good grief, lady, get on your own side of the road!" Tracy swerved to miss the oncoming car, which had drifted into her lane. The remainder of the ninety-minute trip was spent reminiscing about her previous time at the ranch. Michael told her about the new colt and his plans to expand his business by selling his beef directly to markets. They drifted into silence once more.

Tracy was already thinking about the new case and was only half listening. She was curious about Mr. Levine and what led him to America. Every immigrant had a story, some more fascinating than the others. What would Mr. Levine's story be?

Tracy parked the car and pushed the button, opening the hatch. Michael retrieved his bag and they walked into the airport. She hurried to keep up with him and was relieved when he checked his long stride to match hers. Once inside the airport, Michael walked toward the counter while Tracy settled onto one of the cushioned benches and waited.

"All set?" she asked as Michael rejoined her.

"Piece of cake. Why don't we walk over there behind the pole where we can have a little privacy? I'd like to kiss you goodbye." His large hand held her face gently and he looked at her as if memorizing every detail. All morning he had been suppressing the gut feeling that the quality of their relationship was diminishing. Now, that feeling reared its ugly head even stronger.

"I hope it won't be too long before we see each other again."

"Me, too." She didn't miss his obvious examination and she felt a certain sadness that their time together had ended so soon. Parting her lips, she raised herself to meet his kiss.

Michael kissed her, lingering, savoring every moment as if it would be the last kiss. Finally, raising his mouth from hers, he gazed into her eyes. "I suppose that will have to do for a while. Please don't let it be too long, Tracy." He turned without a backward glance and was gone.

Tracy stood in lonely silence and watched Michael as he cleared the security checkpoint. She suddenly felt guilty she hadn't spent more quality time with him. That must have been what was wrong with Michael, she mused. Perhaps he felt rejected and rightly so. The brief two days of his visit, she had to work in the shop because Amy had a touch of something causing an upset stomach, then she had to organize deliveries and return calls. There had been little free time in her busy schedule. So wrapped up in thought, Tracy bumped into an elderly man almost knocking him down.

"I'm so sorry." She reached out to help him, but he just straightened his hat and walked on, not even acknowledging her apology. "Must be on an important mission." At least, moving like he was, he didn't seem to be hurt.

As she left the airport, Tracy called home and checked her messages. Mrs. Bidwell's voice was the first Tracy heard, and she seemed anxious for Tracy to come by. She returned the landlady's call on her way back and decided she would make the apartment complex her first stop.

The lots near the ocean where Tracy lived, as in other beach towns, were small and filled with colorful, well-kept cottages. Back yards were literally the beach and front yards were almost non-existent except for short driveways. Her home, along with several others, was just at the beginning of the development and still zoned for business.

In the center of town where Mr. Levine's apartment was located, however, were the older communities of apartments and older homes turned into duplexes. With the University nearby, there was rarely a vacancy in this area.

Tracy slowed her car and checked addresses on the buildings. When she found the right one, she eased into the next parking space.

Some of the buildings along this street were similar to the brownstones seen in movies about New York, while others were two and three story apartment buildings. They were neat but definitely showing their age; efforts at keeping them in good repair were evidenced by new patches of paint. The paint was closely matched to the original, but created a dappled effect on some. Mature trees lined the street giving a respite from the heat, which seemed to be exceptional this year. Fortunately, at home, Tracy had the ocean breezes to keep her cool.

She twisted her long brown hair into a ponytail and reached into the console for something with which to secure it. Glancing in the mirror, she smoothed the stray wisps behind her ears. At least that would keep the hair off her neck and be cooler.

Two young men coming down the sidewalk slowed their steps and watched as she fixed her hair. One said something to the other and they laughed. When she stepped from the car, they stood in front of her and blocked her way. As she tried to get around them, one man remained in front of her and the other stepped behind. Tracy said nothing; she stood her ground waiting for their next move. The man in front reached over, crooked a finger and ran the knuckle down the side of her face. Still, she didn't move. Finally the young man said boldly, "Hey baby, I'd like to get into your pants."

Tracy looked him straight in the eye and retorted, "Why, did you shit in yours?"

Her question caught him off guard and his mouth dropped open in shock. His intended intimidation had backfired. Such a response had been unexpected, especially from a woman who obviously had class. Her clothing and the expensive SUV she drove spoke volumes to them.

Tracy walked around him and climbed the steps. At the top she hesitated and withdrew her cell phone. "Hey guys," she called to the young men still standing on the sidewalk. When they looked her way, she snapped their picture. "Thanks, now if anything is wrong with my car when I come out— a scratch, a low tire, anything— I'll know who to look for. And, guys, you don't want me looking for you. Take my word on that."

She turned around and pushed the button marked "manager," announcing herself when a voice required her identity. A buzzing sound, followed by a click, indicated the door had been unlocked. Tracy stood a minute to let her eyes adjust to the darkness in the hall.

"Miss Chandler?" Mrs. Bidwell called. "Back here."

Tracy couldn't see the manager but followed the sound of her voice. A variety of noises could be heard coming from the apartments as she passed by—a baby's cry, a television game show Tracy recognized from years ago. Somewhere a phone rang. The scents, accumulated from years of meals cooked, cigarette and cigar smoke, mixed with odors best left alone, were just as varied.

The apartment was down the hall and around the corner, hidden by a staircase. Mrs. Bidwell closed her door and locked it and then motioned to the stairs behind her.

Small in stature and thin, Agnes Bidwell's white hair twisted neatly into a knot on top of her head, did little to add height. Her sharply pointed nose supported wire-rim, no frills-eyeglasses. The pristine white apron, which looped around her neck and tied about her waist, hugged her body and hid much of the simple black dress she wore. Her shoes and stockings were also black.

"Mr. Levine's apartment is one flight up. He's paid up for the rest of the month, but I have someone interested in it. Of course, they wouldn't move in until the first of next month, but I have to clean it and get it ready." She paused on the steps and looked back at Tracy. "You will be able to remove his things before then, won't you? I can't afford to have an empty apartment for very long."

"Well, it depends on how much he has and how long it takes to inventory it. You'll need to verify the inventory once it's done. I'll move it to my warehouse until such time we can locate a relative."

The one bedroom apartment was neat and sparsely furnished. The living room held an ancient couch, a recliner— the one newer item— and a desk. There was no dining room, but the kitchen provided enough space for a small breakfast area. There a red dinette set trimmed in chrome and two matching chairs, shared the space with a refrigerator and stove. The latter two items stayed with the apartment. A bed, nightstand and chest of drawers, equally old, furnished the bedroom.

"How much do you know about Mr. Levine?"

"Only what he had listed on his application. He kept pretty much to himself."

"How long did he live here?" Tracy asked, turning toward the desk in the front room.

"Eighteen years."

"Have you been here that long as well?"

"I've been here twenty-five years."

"Did he ever have visitors?"

"None that I saw, but then I don't have time to watch the comings and goings of my tenants' visitors," Mrs. Bidwell answered curtly. "I told all this to the police when they came around."

"I guess they didn't find any papers or personal effects, like photographs that would reveal anything about a family." Tracy addressed this statement more to herself than to the manager.

"No, ma'am. The police looked around but didn't find anything other than his passport. He was a frugal man. Not many possessions."

"I can see that," Tracy acknowledged as she approached the desk. The antique stood against a wall in the living room. A flat front piece of wood slanted across the top. When pulled down it made a writing area. There were drawers across the lower half.

"H-m-m-m, this is a nice piece."

She opened each of the larger drawers across the bottom and gently lifted the worn clothing, looking beneath. There was nothing out of the ordinary there. Next she pulled down the top slanted piece, revealing a boxed area with rows of small drawers and a prospect door. She opened each.

"They checked those, too."

"I'm sure they did, but did they check this?" Tracy bent closer and gave a tug on the whole section. The boxed area with the prospect door and the small interior drawers slid out to expose an area hidden at the back. "Bingo!" she exclaimed and pulled out a slim, leather bound book, two photographs and several letters. Most letters were stamped "return to sender."

The photos were very old and worn. What appeared to be a young family—mother, father and young daughter—smiled happily from a professional portrait. In the second photo the girl and woman stood in front of a building, maybe a business. Only a portion of the front window was revealed and gave no indication what type of business. An amateur photographer, perhaps the father, had obviously taken this picture.

Tracy picked up the book and examined it closely. Delicate stitching joined the brown, heavily padded cover to the book. The design and lettering on the leather were hand-tooled. A strap held the book together, while a lock at the end of the strap prevented it from being opened. She looked through the drawers and discovered several keys. Trying each, she finally found the right one.

Inside the book were two more letters. She put them with the others to be checked out later. Tracy was more interested in a passport she found in the bottom of the drawer— Mr. Levine's passport. Holes were punched in the document and 'canceled' stamped across the photograph. The picture below the stamp had been taken when he was much younger. She took up the family portrait again and held it next to the passport. The man in the photo was Samuel Levine.

"The passport found by the police— was it current?"

"Yes, the police said his papers were all in order. I was grateful he wasn't here illegally."

"So, he wasn't a citizen after all those years," she mused. Tracy flipped through the first few pages of the book but couldn't read it. The handwritten words were in German and appeared to be a journal, or some kind of record- keeping book. Tracy's knowledge of the language was very limited, to say the least. She could bless someone if they sneezed, or ask in German if they spoke English, but that was about it.

Jean Lindeman, her dear friend who taught at the local college, knew the language well. Her mother was from Germany and she grew up with the language spoken in her household.

"I'll take this and see if I can find out anything about his family. We'll put it on the top of the inventory list. Will that be all right with you?"

"Sure, but if you don't find anyone, what will become of his belongings?" Her question seemed more than idle curiosity. She stared at the desk, a look of newfound appreciation for the antique piece of furniture.

"They will be turned over to the state and auctioned off once it's been decided he has no living relatives. Or, as I'm sure you know, you can go to the court and start proceedings to move the furniture into storage for the legal amount of time and if no one claims it then, you can do the paperwork to gain possession of it."

"How would I know? I've never had anyone die in my building," she mumbled.

Tracy picked up the letters and examined them. A couple were postmarked 1939 and sent to Lyon, France. Those addressed to a Mrs.

Samuel Levine, perhaps his wife or mother, were the ones not returned to the sender. There were two more. One from Shanghai was open and when Tracy checked it, the date Samuel had written on the top was April 14,1939. It had never been mailed. The other, postmarked 1948, originated in San Diego and had been sent to South Dakota. The latter one was marked "return to sender". Both were addressed to Miss Hannah Levine. *Was that the daughter she saw in the photograph? What became of these people and how did Mr. Levine get separated from them?*

The last letter in the book was addressed to Mr. and Mrs. Sidney Steinfeld in South Dakota. Why was that kept in a different place? Who were these people to Samuel? Maybe the book would answer some of those questions. She was anxious to take it to her friend. Checking her watch, Tracy calculated that if she hurried she could catch Jean before her students returned from lunch.

"This is good stuff, Tracy. Where did you get it?" Professor Lindeman exclaimed. The excitement added shine to her hazel eyes. "It's like reading a history book."

"What does it say? Tell me."

"It's a journal and it starts in 1938 Germany. Wow, what a find!"

"Read it to me, Jean."

"Well, let's see."

1938, November 10—

It is getting more dangerous here every day. Last night the Gestapo broke the windows of mine and many of my fellow Jewish shop owners and looted some merchandise. The items in my store were of no consequence (I had planned well in advance for this happening). More as another way to intimidate us rather than put us completely out of business. Earlier today SS officers started rounding up Jews in my neighborhood. We were able to pack a few things and prepare for a journey of which neither of us knew its length or duration. Tonight, I put my family on the train for freedom and safety. They will travel to Heilbronn, where they will be met by sympathizers and taken to Lyon, France. They will stay in France until it is safe to come home again.

"I remember reading about this. They called it 'Kristallnacht', Night of the Broken Glass. Young Nazis went on a rampage, breaking glass in storefronts and killing Jews. Wow, this guy was actually there." Awe-struck, Jean shook her head, a mass of bronze-gold hair inherited from the Irish side of her family, bouncing with the gesture. "I don't mean to make it sound like something to be appreciated. It was a terrible thing that happened that night. I'm just amazed at holding a piece of history here."

"What else does he say? I want to know what happened next."

1938, November 12—

It's getting too dangerous to remain here. I learned today that yesterday and last night some of my people were raped and killed in cold blood and our cemeteries were desecrated. And now there is talk of fines being imposed on all Jewish people. We have been officially boycotted for several years, but enough of the good German citizens ignored the threat from the Government so that most of my fellow shop owners and I could stay in business. Now this. Where will it end and where is the help from the rest of the world?

1938, November 13—

Hopefully, Josef has repaired my old Mercedes. Tonight we must leave the city and find a safe place to stay until spring, and then I will head south to join my family.

1938, Sometime in December—

Josef and I met up with a small caravan of people and have been traveling with them. People are afraid to shelter us in their homes, so we've spent many nights in the woods. It's cold, very cold and especially hard on the younger and older ones among us. We have placed them closer to the fire to stay warm and given them the bulk of the blankets, but one of the little boys is very sick. I will go into the nearby village after sundown and see if I can find a doctor, or at least some medicine.

Students began drifting into the classroom, and reluctantly Jean closed the journal. "Well, darn. I'm so excited about this, but I'm going out of town for a couple of days right after classes. Can you bring it back when I return?" She ran her fingers across the cover, admiring the detail. "I don't want to keep it for fear something will happen to it while I'm gone and I wouldn't dare take it with me." Jean returned the book to Tracy. "It will be nice to read about someone who escaped the

Holocaust, I assume this gentleman did, since he's here. I only hope his family escaped as well."

"That's what I need to find out. Mr. Levine passed away and I have to find his family. No one seems to know much about him. I do have several letters he wrote. They are addressed to his wife and daughter, I think. Those are probably in German also. I wanted to see if the journal would tell us anything before we read the letters."

Tracy gave a disappointed sigh and tucked the journal into her briefcase, after wrapping it in a protective cloth. She would put this in her safe at the bank. Something this old and important needed to be in a protected location to prevent damage, or theft. She didn't want to take the chance she would lose the book, either.

"I'll call you when I get back."

"The time will pass quickly, I suppose. There's a lot to do while you're gone. Call me the *minute* you get back into town." Tracy swept an errant strand of hair behind her ear, a habit she had acquired when stressed. She hugged Jean and she left the classroom.

Across the front of Tracy's house were two doors and a series of three garage doors. The door to the far left opened into her antique shop. The garage doors were on the far right. The middle door opened to steep stairs that climbed up to a landing. There, a door to the right led to her private quarters. The stairwell could also be reached from the shop and garage.

Tracy entered the stairwell from the garage. She bent down and picked up the mail, which had been pushed through the slot in the middle door. With the heel of one foot she shoved the door closed behind her and walked up stairs. Turning the key in the door to her living quarters, she jiggled it ever so gently. The door had been installed a couple of years earlier, along with the wall enclosing the staircase. Before, the stairs descended right into the antique shop and a customer found his way up to her living quarters. Something happened to the lock at that time. Either it was installed off kilter, or damaged in some way; she never had it fixed.

Tracy could see the message light flashing on her answering machine as she walked down the hallway and into her bedroom. She pushed the button and Michael's voice filled the air.

"Hi, Tracy. Finally got home and I miss you already. Call me when you get in." The machine beeped and another message began.

"Hello, this is Agnes Bidwell. Please call me as soon as possible. Thank you."

Tracy kicked off her shoes and then picked up the phone and dialed Michael's number. Her stomach rumbled. It was three o'clock in the afternoon and she realized she had not eaten lunch. While the call was connecting, she went into the kitchen and opened the fridge door.

"Hello, Michael here."

"Just the fellow I was looking for," Tracy answered, lowering her voice and being purposefully mysterious. "What are you wearing right now? Something brief and sexy?"

"Ah, and wouldn't you like to know?" His laugh was low and throaty. "Come over and find out for yourself."

"How was your trip?" She asked, changing the subject.

"Long and tiring. And how was your fact-finding mission?"

"Quite interesting, actually." Tracy went into detail about Mrs. Bidwell and finding the journal. She related what Jean had revealed from the journal, and her disappointment in not being able to find out more until the professor's return.

"I'm envious. What a great find. What's your next move?"

"I'm going to go on line and check out the Ellis Island Web page. I want to see if Samuel's wife and daughter made it to America together. I have letters he sent them in France and some sent to South Dakota, but the South Dakota ones are addressed only to a Miss Hannah Levine in care of Steinfeld and mailed once he got to the States. I assume Hannah's the daughter. Obviously they were never delivered since I have them now. The letters came back to him. I don't know if the people in South Dakota are relatives or not. If so, how did he lose track of them? Why was his daughter with them and where was Mrs. Levine? Maybe the information will be noted somewhere in the journal. "

"I'm sure you'll find all that out," Michael assured her. "I have every bit of confidence in you."

"Thanks, Michael, I hope I can." Tracy sighed heavily. "I wonder if he was ever reunited with his family and, if so, how did he lose touch again? It would really be sad if, after he put them on the train, he never saw them again. There are so many questions and so few answers right now." Tracy glanced at her watch and remembered she had to return

Mrs. Bidwell's call. Afterwards she could eat her lunch undisturbed. "Gotta go, Michael. Before I do, I need to apologize to you."

"For what?"

"I'm sorry I was so preoccupied when you were here. I feel badly about that and I hope to make it up to you soon."

Michael was silent for a moment, then, "I'll hold you to that."

"Deal. Talk to you soon. Love you."

"Same here. Keep me informed on your progress."

Tracy hung up the phone. She couldn't remember if the prefix to Mrs. Bidwell's number was 625 or 652, so she checked the notepad in the kitchen and then dialed the correct number.

"Miss Chapman, I'm so glad you called. You need to come over here as soon as possible." There was fear in Agnes Bidwell's voice.

"What's the problem?"

"Just get over here as quick as you can." A click sounded as Mrs. Bidwell disconnected the call.

Tracy spread some peanut butter on a slice of bread, folded it over and took a big bite. She removed a small carton of milk from the refrigerator and gulped it down. Not much of a lunch, but it would have to do for now.

Tracy parked her car and hurried up the landlady's steps. While she waited for Mrs. Bidwell to release the lock, Tracy again wondered what was behind the fear she heard in the manager's voice. She glanced around the building. All seemed quiet. Anxiously she started to push the button again when the squawking sound of the speaker filled the air, startling her. She jerked her hand back.

"Who's there?"

"It's Tracy, Mrs. Bidwell." A buzzing sound followed. She pushed the door open and entered the building. The manager was waiting outside her door and motioned for Tracy to follow her. As they approached Mr. Levine's apartment, Tracy could see red slashes on the door but couldn't make out exactly what they were. Then the image became very clear. A large red swastika had been spray-painted on the door. The evil symbol caused her to gasp aloud.

"Who— when did this happen? Is there any damage inside the apartment?"

"Don't know who and it happened a short time after you left. Whoever it was didn't get inside the apartment itself. Either they were frightened away or — "

"I'll have to move everything out now. Perhaps that will keep anything else from happening." Tracy wasn't convinced, but at least she might prevent further damage to the apartment and stress to Mrs. Bidwell.

"Why would someone do this?" Mrs. Bidwell asked, her voice barely above a whisper.

"To instill terror— maliciousness. Who knows?"

"But Mr. Levine is dead."

"Perhaps it was meant for his family."

"He didn't have any."

"At one time he did and maybe still does," Tracy corrected. "Did you report this to the police?"

"Yes, they came out and made a report. Told me to keep a lookout, but there wasn't much they could do at this point. No one saw anything and there were no fingerprints or anything else to go on. They thought it might be some young people— "

"My, my, what's going on here?" a male voice interrupted, startling both women.

"Who are you and how did you get in?" Mrs. Bidwell asked sharply.

"This is Garth Anderson, the other of Monet Cove's antique dealers," Tracy answered, a tone of sarcasm coloring her voice. Then to Garth, "I didn't notice you circling this time. You're getting better or I'm slipping."

"Chapman, always a pleasure." He bowed mockingly. "What's going on?"

"As you can see for yourself a death can bring out the worst in people, or is it the worst people?" Tracy addressed Mrs. Bidwell.

"Now is that any way to talk about a colleague?"

Tracy ignored the comment, tiring of the verbal jousting. She took out her cell phone and dialed a number. "Vinnie, could you and Harry bring the truck over? I need to move some furniture— no, no heavy stuff and not really a lot of furniture either. Good. Thanks, I owe you— again." Tracy gave him the address and disconnected the call.

"One step ahead of me as usual."

Garth's snide comment didn't escape Tracy. "I'm not buying anything. We have to locate the family. There really isn't anything you would be interested in anyway, except maybe the desk. You'll have a chance at it just like everybody else at the estate sale, unless family members decide to keep everything."

"Can I have a look? It's not that I don't trust you— well, maybe it is, too."

Mrs. Bidwell opened the door and stepped back for Tracy and Garth to enter. "I need to get the door cleaned off and the apartment in order. The person who was going to rent it backed out. He came by to take another look and ask if some of the furniture could stay. His timing was just great. The police were just leaving and of course that thing finished it." She pointed to the blood red swastika. "Hey, who—" She walked quickly down the hall, but by the time she got to the stairs the door below was closing behind a dark figure.

"What's wrong?" Tracy asked, coming up behind her.

"A man was standing on the stairs, his head just high enough to look up the hall here. He hurried off when I saw him."

Tracy ran to the window overlooking the street, but she saw no one. "What did he look like? Have you seen him before?"

"He was an elderly person, but he moved too fast and his back was to me so I didn't get to see his face very good. He wore a dark hat and clothes and had slightly hunched shoulders. I could see bits of white hair beneath the hat. I don't think I've seen him before." Mrs. Bidwell glared at Garth. "How are these people getting in here?"

"I just buzzed one of the tenants and said I locked myself out and a child said he, or she, would let me in. It's hard to tell which from a child's voice. Perhaps he did the same, or maybe the door didn't shut completely when I came in."

"People look through the obituaries to burglarize homes of the deceased. Since Mr. Levine was listed in the phone book, address and all, some of the seedier side of society will most likely be turning up. Hopefully, if they see us moving the furniture out, the apartment will no longer be of interest." Tracy looked out the window again, but still there was no sight of the man.

"I wonder who he was and why he hurried off like that? And did he have any involvement in this sign on the door?" Tracy asked and she checked off a mental list of the past events for possible suspects.

There are several possibilities: either the two thugs I embarrassed earlier today, or this disappearing old man could have been responsible. They might have come back to see if the swastika had been removed and if there was any backlash. On the other hand, maybe one of those radical groups with the shaved heads had painted the door. Then there was Garth— No, he was annoying and obnoxious but never mean spirited.

Aloud, she asked the manager, " Could you send notices around to your tenants not to open the door for anyone they don't personally know? Perhaps this guy will return and we can find out who he is and what his interest is in this place."

"It's in the lease and periodically I post a notice." She grumbled, not happy at being told her job. "I'll post another one."

Tracy turned the corner of her street and drove slowly toward her driveway. The inventory and relocation of Mr. Levine's furniture had taken longer than she thought it would, and the day had been a busy one. With her mind occupied by those events, she suddenly realized she was almost home. It frightened her that she didn't remember most of the trip. *Wow*, she thought, *wonder if I ran any red lights*? She glanced in the rear view mirror. At least the car behind her didn't appear to be one of Monet Cove's finest. Dusk was giving way to nightfall and the headlights prevented Tracy from seeing little more than the shape of the vehicle. It appeared to be a large, dark car and there was no light bar across the top.

Tracy slowed her car even more, hoping the person behind her would go around, but whoever it was just slowed down as well. She lowered her window and motioned for the car to come around, but it did not. Shrugging, she pressed the remote button, and waited as the garage door swung slowly upward. After entering the garage, she watched in her rear view mirror as the other automobile almost came to a stop. When she got out of her car, the other one picked up speed.

"Hm-m-m, that's rather curious." Tracy stood there staring after the red taillights. She watched the car as it turned the corner and disappeared. Unconsciously her brow furrowed. She wondered if this should be a cause for concern. Or was she just being overly dramatic after all that had taken place today? She opted for the latter and hurried inside.

Tracy kicked off her shoes at the living room door, then bent over and picked them up. Carrying them with the heels resting on two fingers, she walked across the room and opened the sliding glass door. The ocean breeze filled the room, blowing the sheer curtains up like an elongated balloon before she could open them.

She took great pleasure in listening to the waves crash ashore. The repetitive, soothing sound followed her down the hall.

Still carrying her shoes, she headed toward her bedroom. The day had been long, filled with many events and emotions. It would probably be well into the night before she could settle down and fall asleep.

Tracy checked the clock radio beside her bed. North Dakota was two hours ahead so it would be ten o'clock there. Michael was most certainly sleeping soundly by now, but she had an overwhelming need to talk to him. Tracy picked up the phone and dialed his number. When he didn't answer on the fourth ring, she almost hung up.

"Hullo." His voice, husky with sleep, could barely be heard over the announcement of his answering machine. "Who is it? Wait a minute."

Tracy heard the sounds as he fought with the machine trying to turn it off, then he was back with her. "Michael, it's me."

"Tracy? What's wrong?" he asked anxiously.

"Nothing. I just wanted to talk to you. To hear your voice."

"Now I know something is wrong."

"Such a comedian at such an hour. How do you do it?" She laughed. "So, how are you? What's going on in your life?"

"Tracy, it's ten o'clock. You didn't call to make small talk. Out with it."

"All right, you win. I did miss you and just wanted to hear your voice. At least that is one thing normal and familiar in my life and makes me feel warm and fuzzy."

"Things not going too well on your new case?" he asked.

"Well, there's been a new development. I'm not sure if it has anything to do with Mr. Levine, or it's just a vicious prank because he was Jewish and from Germany." Tracy explained about the swastika and the attention the apartment was getting. "I'm wondering if there might even be something sinister behind all this. Sometimes two heads are better than one. What do you think?" It was a relief to share her dilemma with someone, especially since Jean was out of town.

"Sounds like you need to get out and let the police handle it. I don't want to see you get hurt— or worse."

"I don't think it's that bad. Besides, the police are going to keep watch in case the culprits try something else. I am perfectly safe. It's just that maybe I'm missing something important and I can't figure out what that might be. The answer might be in the journal, but I won't know for sure until Jean comes back."

"Why don't you come here to see me and take a break?"

"That's out of the question and you know that; people are depending on me. Why don't you come here instead?"

"I was just there as well as the last two times, remember? Anyway, it's kinda hard for me to get away right now."

"Well, talking to you is the next best thing," she sighed. "It'll all work out. I'm sure of it. You go back to sleep and dream nice dreams."

"Oh sure, now that I'm wide awake you're going to run out on me."

"Good night, Michael, pleasant dreams and I miss you." Tracy smiled as she hung up the phone. She had a feeling they would both have trouble finding sleep.

"Tracy, be careful," Michael said, but she was already gone. As he replaced the receiver concern etched deep furrows in his forehead.

Chapter Three

The next morning, while Tracy was in the shower, she thought she heard the phone. She stuck her head out and listened intently, but the noise of the running water still made it difficult to be certain. Quickly, she turned the water off and listened again. It *was* the phone. She grabbed a towel, wrapping it firmly around her, but before she could reach it, the answering machine picked up the call.

"Hi, Tracy, Jean here. My trip back has been delayed for another day. Hope you are out on some marvelous adventure. See you when I get home."

Although she was disappointed that she would have to wait longer to learn more about the journal, the sound of her best friend's voice made Tracy smile. They were really more like sisters than friends and had been since they were roommates in college. After she married the dean of a city college in San Francisco, Jean moved away for ten years. When her marriage ended in a bitter divorce five years later, Jean moved back, acquiring a position at the same college she and Tracy had attended in Monet Cove.

Jean was the more sensible of the two and often counseled Tracy on her many daring escapades while they were in college. Again Tracy smiled as she dressed to go to the gym.

The Kickboxing tournament was a little more than two weeks away now, and she needed to get in some practice if she was to do better this go-round. First place had eluded her in the past and she was determined to make it this time. She glanced at her watch and hurried into the kitchen. Breakfast would be a cold Pop Tart this morning and she promised herself a more nutritious lunch.

Tracy had only an hour to work out and then she had to go to the warehouse to check Mr. Levine's desk again. She wanted to make sure there was nothing else to add to his story. Earlier, after finding the journal, she had looked no further. Perhaps she had skipped something.

Later she would check with Mrs. Bidwell to see if anything else happened regarding Mr. Levine's apartment, and then go home to check out the Ellis Island website. Hopefully, somewhere in there she could talk with Amy and see how the search for the second shop location was going.

The current antique shop was outgrowing its space beneath her house and rather than closing it and finding a larger building, Tracy decided to open a second one at the center of town. With a population of 111,500 full time residents and students and all the tourists that frequented the town, Monet Cove was big enough to support two shops, three including Garth's. Since locals and die-hard antique collectors frequented the one beneath her home, she would keep the bigger and more expensive pieces here.

The phone rang abruptly, startling her. Tracy was torn between going out the door and answering the call. If she answered the phone, she might not accomplish her goals set for the day; she was sure of that, but her curiosity got the better of her.

"Hi Trace," Amy greeted cheerfully. "I have a customer on the phone who wants to know if we got any new items in the past day or so. I told him I didn't think so, but he seemed to think otherwise. He asked me to check and make sure."

"No," Tracy answered. Then an alarm went off in Tracy's head. "This customer wouldn't happen to be an old man, would it? Does he sound elderly?"

"Yes, as a matter of fact he does. How did you know?"

"See if you can get a name and phone number and tell him we will call him back. Anything else about him I should know?" If this was the guy from the apartment, she wanted a name so she could do some research on him.

"He has a heavy German accent."

"Keep him on the line. I'll be right down." She was sure now that man on the phone was the one who had been at the apartment. *Why else would he be so insistent that we had new merchandise? He had probably been somewhere nearby watching them remove the furniture. And since he spoke with a German accent, he might just be connected in some way to Samuel. It couldn't be a coincidence, could it?*

Tracy ran down the steps two at a time, unlocked the door and rushed to the front of the shop. To her dismay Amy shrugged her shoulders and shook her head.

"Sorry, I couldn't hold him. He said he would call back in a few days. Wouldn't leave a name or phone number. I did the last number recall and there was no number available."

"I'm almost sure he is the person who showed up at Mr. Levine's apartment yesterday. Why is he being so evasive?" She addressed the question more to herself as she turned to go back upstairs. Abruptly, she stopped in mid-stride and turned around, "Amy, keep a look out and if he comes in, please get in touch with me as quickly as possible. I'll have my cell phone on at all times. Make up some excuse to keep him here. I have to find out if he is connected to Mr. Levine, or if he saw the obit in the newspaper and is just curious about a fellow countryman."

Tracy pushed a lock of hair behind her ear and picked up the phone, dialing Mrs. Bidwell's number. "Hi, Mrs. Bidwell, this is Tracy. How are you doing? Good. No further incidents, I hope. Well, that's good news. Did that old fellow happen to come back?" Tracy frowned and switched the phone to her other ear. "If he does, will you try to find out his name and what he wants? I'd sure appreciate that. If you need me for anything please don't hesitate to call. Thanks, Mrs. Bidwell." She gave the manager her cell phone number. In case he decided to pay a visit, Tracy didn't want Mrs. Bidwell to call her house and leave a message because she wasn't sure when she would be home to get it.

She groaned. There wouldn't be time to practice her kickboxing today. She definitely wanted to check the antique desk again and see if there was anything there to shed some light on this new mystery. Tracy waved to Amy as she ran back upstairs to get her bag and keys. Coming back down, she took the opposite door, completely forgetting to speak with Amy about the search for a new shop.

Tracy looked in both directions as she backed out to see if the car from the night before might be parked somewhere waiting to follow her. How silly. She mentally reprimanded herself for being overly suspicious and headed toward town.

The late morning sun was bright as Tracy drove down Central Street toward the warehouse. Small cafes, tee shirt and curio shops were abundant along Central. A steady stream of tourists flowed down the sidewalks, some stopping occasionally to inspect a rack of tee shirts, or peer into the shop windows at curios. Others sat at sidewalk cafes at umbrella-covered tables sipping their favorite beverages watching the world go by.

Tracy pushed the button on the car door and the window whirred down. A multitude of heavenly scents filled her car. There was everything from sea air to a blend of various ethnic foods being prepared for the lunch hour. Her stomach growled, protesting the cold toaster pastry she had gulped down for breakfast. She swung her car into the parking lot of a pizza restaurant where a large banner advertised a lunch buffet. It was a few minutes past eleven. Hopefully, she would be just ahead of the crowd.

Pushing the door open, Tracy went inside. The place already had numerous customers, even at the early hour, and she started to leave. When her stomach rumbled again, she walked up to the podium instead and gave the young girl her name for the waiting list.

"How long?"

"Only a couple of minutes. How many in your party?"

"Just me. Thanks."

"Oh, a table has just opened up. Will you follow me, please?"

The table overlooked the parking lot. As she sat down, Tracy glanced toward her SUV just in time to see the two young men from Mr. Levine's neighborhood pull in beside it. They got out and looked at her vehicle, then toward the building. Curious about their intentions, she leaned back behind the window frame so they couldn't see her.

One man got back in their vehicle on the passenger side, while the other one headed for the restaurant. Inside, he looked around trying to be inconspicuous. Tracy watched him over the menu. He spotted her just as the hostess approached him and he jerked his head around, startled by her voice. He leaned close to her and said something. After she reached behind the podium and handed him a take-out menu, he left the building. Once outside, he got into the driver's side of the car and backed out, parking a few spaces down.

Tracy returned her attention to the menu, glancing at the options. She decided on the buffet and calmly strolled in that direction. She was hungry, having skipped too many meals already, so she certainly wasn't going to forego her lunch for these guys. *They can just cool their heels and wait for me.*

Later, with her meal finished, she checked on her "new best friends" outside; they were still there. Leaving the restaurant, she made her way to the driver's side of their vehicle. Its windows were down and they were arguing over something. Neither saw her walk up.

"Hey there, what a surprise. You guys aren't waiting for me are you?"

The driver swore under his breath as he turned on the ignition and burned rubber backing out of the space. As he sped off, Tracy could see that the two men appeared to be yelling at each other. Smiling, she went to her car. She still had to check out the desk, then go home to research the Ellis Island Website.

She was almost sure Mr. Levine's daughter had made it to the United States because of the letters addressed to a Miss Hannah Levine in South Dakota. *But what happened to Mrs. Levine? Did his wife make it to America with their daughter, and did Mr. Levine follow later?*

Was he at odds with his wife, or had he been in touch with her and the letters got through? If so, what happened and why was he in California alone? Was there a divorce? Tracy would check to see if he had papers in the desk that she hadn't come across. *Possibly mixed in with his clothes,* she thought. She hadn't checked those thoroughly. So many questions, so few answers.

But Mr. Levine's desk gave up no more clues about the family, much to Tracy's dismay. No legal papers in his clothing drawers, either. She checked every cubbyhole twice but there was nothing. *All the family's belongings— pictures, personal effects and the like—must be with the other family members. Mr. Levine certainly didn't take any of those things with him when he fled their home, only the two photographs I found previously.*

Tracy's fingers rubbed circles against her temples. The skipped meals were taking their toll, causing a low-blood-sugar headache. Hopefully, the lunch a short time ago would counteract that condition before the headache got too severe.

She closed up the desk, locked it and looked at her watch. By the time she stopped at the market, picked up some groceries and got home, Amy would be gone for the day. Tomorrow morning she would make a point to sit down with her and find out how the search for a building, and an employee to man it, was coming along.

When Tracy locked up the warehouse and started for her car, her cell phone rang. She held up the phone and groaned when she saw the name displayed. *What does he want*?

"Garth, to what do I owe this honor?"

"Just wondered how things were going with your latest conquest. Have you found any relatives?"

"Which conquest would that be?"

"Don't be coy, Chapman, you know which one I mean."

"Sorry to disappoint you, but no, nothing to report. You will be the first to know after me, though."

"Any more trouble?"

"Nothing that I can't handle."

"Look, you could be dealing with a pretty rough bunch, Chapman. Don't go risking that pretty neck of yours."

"Don't tell me you are worried about me, Garth."

"I'm serious, Tracy. That nasty paint job might have just been a prank, but if it wasn't— just be careful."

Tracy's left eyebrow rose a fraction. Theirs had been a relationship of business rivalry over the years, not necessarily hostile, although not friendly either. To keep her aware of that fact, Garth rarely used her first name. Caught off guard, she suddenly regretted her flippancy. His concern seemed genuine, so she hesitated before speaking again, not wanting to say anything to diminish his thoughtfulness.

"Thanks, Garth, I— "

"Hold on a minute." Garth's voice lowered and he spoke angrily to someone with him. "A hundred on Ring of Fire— You heard what I said. Okay? Okay." There was silence, then, "Are you there, Chapman?"

"Yes, I'm here. Sounds like you have a bidding war going on there. I hope the Ring of Fire is something really special."

"Yeah, me, too."

" Listen, I appreciate your concern, but I can assure you I am okay."

After an awkward silence, he ended their brief conversation. "Good. Well, I guess I'll see you around."

Tracy didn't know quite what to make of the phone call. She wouldn't necessarily characterize Garth as being considerate, but then she didn't really know a whole lot about him. He wasn't a bad looking fellow; pleasant looking would be more the way she would describe him. He was tall, a little over six feet, and a bit on the lanky side. He always dressed nicely, choosing colors to compliment his brown hair and eyes. His best feature, though, was his lop-sided smile punctuated by a whisper of dimples.

A blaring horn brought Tracy's attention back from her reverie. She glanced around but couldn't see what prompted the horn blowing. She shrugged her shoulders and headed once again to her vehicle. Too many things to do and not enough time, she thought.

Backing out of the parking space, she turned into the stream of traffic. The street climbed north before connecting with the coast highway and then curved and snaked around the hills toward her home and the cliffs just beyond.

Tracy touched a button and lowered her window once again. This time of the year, early summer before it got too hot, was her favorite, when the wild flowers colored the cliffs leading down to the ocean. The scent of sea air filled her car and the wind, as it whipped at her hair, made her sigh heavily. She reached up and tucked a strand behind her ear only to have it blow free again. Reluctantly, she pushed the button and raised the window. There were curves ahead and she wanted a clear line of vision in case some fool decided to pass where it was dangerous to do so. There was always that one who considered rules were for others. Twice this month already there had been collisions; one was fatal.

In her rear view mirror, Tracy noticed the car coming up at a fast rate and it didn't appear to slow down as it neared her. He was obviously in a big hurry and intended to pass. There was no place to pull over, so she pressed the accelerator. The car closed in and Tracy picked up more speed. Her car swerved into the oncoming traffic lane as she went around a curve. Fortunately there was no traffic in that lane. She corrected slightly. She glanced briefly at her rear view mirror to see the driver. It was a man, that much she could tell, but she had to keep her attention on the road. To do otherwise would be to risk missing a curve, or hitting an oncoming motorist.

Whump! The vehicle tapped her bumper. Tracy swerved once more, then dragged the wheel back. Again he tapped her car, sending it into the oncoming lane. Another car was coming toward her. She jerked her car back, narrowly missing it, but the maneuver caused her vehicle to fishtail. She fought to gain control. The driver of the oncoming car leaned on his horn and shouted an obscenity at her as he went past.

The attack car fell back when she swerved, but now the driver closed the distance and he nudged her car again. They were coming into a residential neighborhood near her house. Tracy began honking her horn, hoping to attract attention. If nothing else she could at least warn people to get out of the way. Where were the police when you needed them?

She passed the turn off to her house and was traveling toward the cliffs, where the road became even more dangerous. Suddenly, the other driver slammed on his brakes, laying down skid marks. Smoke billowed from the back of his vehicle and the smell of burned rubber filled the air. He made a u-turn and sped away. Tracy slowed her own vehicle and pulled to the side of the road. She sat there, shaking and trying to compose herself. That man tried to kill her!

When she stopped shaking Tracy pulled her cell phone out and dialed 911. "I want to report an accident— no, there are no injuries, but the other driver left the scene." Tracy gave her location and within minutes a police cruiser arrived.

"Are you hurt, Miss Chapman?"

"No, just shook up. I'm not sure it was an accident though, Officer—Officer Henry isn't it?" He nodded as Tracy told him what had occurred. "There isn't much I can tell you about the other driver. I was pretty busy trying to stay alive, but the car was an older model tan Jeep."

"Did you get any part of the license plate number?"

"Sorry. Things got pretty dicey and then he just backed off and went the other way."

Mike Henry filled out the report and handed a copy to Tracy. "If you think of anything else, or you see this Jeep around town, give me a call. If by chance you do see it, try to get the plate number. Don't attempt to take him on yourself. From the sounds of it I think you were right. It appears he might have been trying to kill you. And you don't know who he was?"

"No, and I don't know why he did it, either."

"Well, we'll have an officer swing by your house once in a while and check on things." He examined the rear of her car. "Doesn't look like the damage will affect the operation of your vehicle, but you should call a tow truck. You have no brake lights and the bumper is barely hanging on."

"I'll do that. Thanks. Is that all?"

"For now. If we locate the vehicle we'll notify you." He touched the brim of his hat and left.

Tracy started the engine, turned her car around and eased into the far lane. She decided not to mention the incident to anyone else, but she was certainly going to be watching her back more closely from now on.

She drove slowly down the hill and turned on to her street. She would call the tow truck from home. At least she could be working, instead of spending time stuck at the garage. The sound of metal scraping the blacktop made her cringe. Tracy sat straight in her seat as though that would keep the bumper from dragging. She turned up the car radio volume, blocking out the scraping noise.

Chapter Four

Tracy had been on line at the Ellis Island Website for over an hour and only located Samuel's entry into the United States. There was no mention of a Hannah Levine and, since she didn't have the first name of Mrs. Levine, there was no way of tracking the wife. It had been hard enough to locate Samuel. One needed name, age at arrival, date of arrival, and port of embarkation or departure. While she didn't have the port of departure to enter, she had his birth date and the date of arrival in New York. He entered the country in 1939. She was pleased she had paid close attention to his old passport before locking it away for safekeeping.

Returning to the page of photographs, she studied them closely and was struck by hard times etched upon the immigrants' faces. The caption under the photograph indicated these people were headed for the inspection room. There the immigrants were inspected for disease and defects before being allowed to enter the United States. They looked so bewildered and tired. Tracy supposed they were also afraid of the examinations ahead of them. How humiliating those must have been.

In other photographs, children clung to their mothers. Some were in their mother's arms, others standing by their side and clutching a dress or coattail. Her belongings wrapped in a bundle balanced on her head, one mother and her children stood apart from the others, appearing dazed at what they had already been through, or what was yet to come. Her son on her left side, dressed in a rumpled suit and hat, held his younger sibling. On the other side stood the daughter, a large bundle under her arm.

Another photo showed a ship coming into the harbor, every inch of its deck was covered with passengers. There was hardly space to move. What courage it had taken to leave their homes and journey to a foreign land. Most probably had no knowledge of the language, or what they would be facing. What was in their minds as they crowded together and watched our lovely Lady Liberty slip into view? What lay ahead for these people? She wondered if Samuel Levine was in any of the pictures.

At least Tracy had the address of the Steinfelds. It was the one on the envelopes addressed to Hannah in South Dakota. That was so long ago, but it would be a place to start. She could look up the family on a website which listed just about everybody in the United States, along with their age, address and phone number.

Tracy stretched and rubbed her eyes. She shut down the computer and glanced at the clock, nine thirty. Where did the time go? Tracy smiled as she recalled another time she asked the same thing. She had been working with the nuns at St. Joseph's Cathedral, helping organize their annual rummage sale to benefit the homeless families up and down the coast. Having lost track of the time, the hours seemed to have flown by and she asked that question. Sister Mary Catherine answered, "Into eternity, dear, into eternity." Her answer so impressed Tracy that she never forgot it.

Stretching again, she wandered into the kitchen. Picking the carton of milk from the refrigerator, she shook it to determine how much was left. "Should have gotten more milk at the store," she said aloud. Tracy opened the carton, pulled out the spout and finished it. A small amount dribbled onto her chin. She used the back of her hand to wipe it off, then went to the sink and rinsed out the carton. Crumpling the carton flat, she tossed it into the trash. Tracy went back through the living room and stepped out onto the deck.

Leaning against the railing, Tracy stared out into the moonlight. The full moon painted silver on the water and made the white foamy waves breaking against the shore glow. The ocean breeze was cold and damp, though, making Tracy shiver, but she stayed outside and continued to stare. She needed to quiet her thoughts before going to bed and the sound of the surf was consoling.

There were few people on the beach at that hour as it was a private section. Cole Sanders, her neighbor from two doors down, was one.

He called and waved to her as he jogged past. Because he usually didn't get home from work until nine or nine-thirty, Cole often jogged with his Dalmatian, Beau, late at night during the summer. Tracy wasn't sure what he did for a living that kept him away so late. The few times she had shared a conversation with him they never got around to discussing their respective careers.

Tracy turned and was about to go back inside when a slight movement in the darkness caught her attention. She stood still, straining her eyes to get a closer look, but she could see nothing. Back inside, she shivered and rubbed her arms vigorously after shutting the door.

Two figures clothed in black blended into the night, becoming all but invisible. Cole Sanders almost collided with them. They mumbled something and hurried past him, stopping at a spot farther up the beach where they could still watch Tracy's house. When the lights went out, one of the figures pushed a button on his watch and checked the time.

"We'll wait an hour. By then she should be sound asleep."

"Half an hour," the other one interjected. "Who lays in bed an hour before they go to sleep?"

"Well, obviously not you."

Tracy went into the bedroom and checked her answering machine to make sure there had been no calls while she was on the deck. No messages. She walked into her closet and took off her clothes. Removing the much worn dorm shirt from the back of her closet door, she slipped it over her head. *Should get rid of this thing before it falls apart*, she mused, *but it's just at that comfortable stage*. There were two full drawers of sleepwear, some of which had never been worn; only a few she actually used. This one was her favorite.

She switched on the bedside lamp and picked up a book lying on the table. With all she had on her mind, Tracy really wasn't that tired. Perhaps if she read for a while, she wouldn't lie there going over work related issues.

When the light came on, one of the watchers uttered, "Shit," and turned to his companion. "Marcos, how long do you think before the broad gets in bed?"

"What do I look like, a psychic? How the hell should I know?"

"Well, I think we should ask for more money." He lifted one foot and took off his shoe, shaking it upside down. "I got sand in my shoes and probably other places, too. I hate the beach. I hate waiting around."

"Aw, quit your whining, Jack. I'm not about to ask for more money. That old dude is one cold, mean bastard, besides he's upset with us already because we haven't finished our job yet."

"And you had to go and— "

Just then the light went off in Tracy's bedroom and Marcos checked his watch again. "We'll time it from now. Half an hour should do it."

Tracy had read the same paragraph three times. After turning off the light, she put the book back on her nightstand. Her mind was too active and she couldn't concentrate on the plot. She shifted around in bed trying to get comfortable. Perhaps if she just lay there in the darkness and kept her eyes closed, sleep would come. She tossed and turned a few minutes, then angrily flung the sheet back and got out of bed. *Maybe if I take some aspirin—*

Not bothering to turn on lights again, Tracy followed the glow from the bathroom night-light. She was wide-awake enough without making it any worse by turning on lights. After retrieving a glass from the kitchen cabinet, she went back to the bathroom. Tracy filled the glass with water from the faucet and shook two aspirin from the bottle, swallowing them.

Tracy closed the bathroom door and crawled into bed once more. Immediately her mind began unsuccessfully to seek out solutions to the problems building the past few days. *Where was the daughter? Was she even alive? When would Jean return and would she be able to find the answers in the journal?*

Minutes passed. It was now eleven o'clock and still sleep did not come; she wasn't even tired yet. Tracy sat up and plumped her pillow with her fists then fell back down, only to toss and turn. Finally, she got up and went back into the kitchen to warm a glass of milk. Maybe that would make her drowsy enough to fall asleep. Certainly, nothing else was working. *Darn, I forgot. I used the last of it!* At that moment she heard a noise coming from—where? She listened carefully, holding her breath as if that would make her hear better. There it was! Someone was trying to get in the storeroom's back door downstairs, right below the kitchen.

Had she turned on the alarm? Quietly, she slipped into the living room and checked the controls. Yes, thank goodness she had the sense to do that, but it was almost an automatic thing with her. So automatic, in fact she rarely remembered setting the thing.

Next, Tracy lay down on the floor and strained her ears. The noise grew a little louder and she heard a click as the door below was opened. The alarm was a silent one and would notify the company. The dispatcher would then call to make sure it was not an error on her part. Pushing up from the floor, she quickly made her way to the phone so she could pick it up at the first ring. Tracy didn't want the intruder scared away before the police arrived.

"Someone has just broken in downstairs," she whispered into the phone.

"We'll notify the police right away. Stay on the line with me," the man instructed her, but Tracy had already put the phone down.

Tracy eased the door to the stairway open and listened. He hadn't breached the door leading upstairs and she guessed he probably wouldn't. After all, she assumed he was a burglar and the store was full of very expensive objects. She had time to get downstairs and into the garage. There was a side door leading outside which she planned to unlock and let the police in. They should arrive any minute now.

Quietly, she descended the dark stairwell and hesitated at the shop door, listening. Her hand reached for the lock, but she decided to go with her first plan. She could handle one person, but there was no way to know how many were in there. *Best if I let the police handle it*, she thought.

As the door opened into the garage, the hinges squeaked and the sound seemed to explode in the silence. She paused. There was no sound in the other room. Tracy was not sure if the intruder heard her and didn't want to wait just in case. Feeling her way in the darkness, she moved as quickly as she could through the garage and around her car.

Meantime, in the shop, Marcos had heard the squeaking hinge. He signaled to Jack motioning him to the garage door. He took out a credit card and with a quick swipe immediately had the shop door unlocked. The two men were in the garage before Tracy had time to get out. Jack ran his hand along the wall feeling for the light switch without success. He reached out and grabbed Marcos, signaling him to wait.

Having heard the intruders enter the garage, Tracy stood as still and quietly as she could. Her eyes were beginning to adjust to the darkness and she could see two dark-colored shapes near the door. For a time she heard nothing but her heart beating. She was certain they could hear her breathing as well.

A third section of the garage was all that stood between her and the outside door, but that side was filled with boxes full of merchandise. She would have to be careful. But as she took a step she tripped over one of crates. At that same time the intruders found the light switch. Scrambling to get up, Tracy squinted against the bright light, giving Jack and Marcos the chance to catch her.

They got on either side, picked her up under her arms, and slammed her against the back wall of the garage. Her feet dangled just above the floor. They held her pinned to the wall. Jack took advantage of the situation and pressed against her, grinding his body into hers. His lips twisted into a cynical smile. "Not so uppity now, huh?"

Alarm and anger rippled along her spine. She twisted her face away from him as he brought his lips down toward hers. "This the only way you can get a girl?"

Jack raised his hand to slap her across the face, but Marcos grabbed his wrist. "Leave it alone. We came for something else." He turned his attention to Tracy and demanded, "Okay, Miss High and Mighty, tell us where the old man's stuff is?" Marcos' dark eyes narrowed as he waited for an answer.

"What old man are you talking about?" she asked, trying to stall until the police arrived.

Jack got right in her face and spoke through clenched teeth, "Okay smart mouth bitch, you aren't going to get away with it this time." His eyes narrowed, "Too bad I couldn't finish the job yesterday; you'd have been knocking at the pearly gates by now."

"Ah, was that you in the jeep? The one who chickened out? Did you do that on purpose, or do you just lose control of everything you do?"

Jack moved in front of her, raising his free hand again to strike her. She ducked her head and he slapped the wall next to her. This was the break Tracy needed. In a flash she swung one foot up and kicked Jack in the groin, causing him to drop immediately to the ground. She landed another kick, this one to Marcos' nose. He grabbed his nose, blood gushing through his fingers. Tracy quickly jumped across the floor and hit the button to raise the garage door. Marcos fled, leaving Jack groaning in pain on the floor.

Within seconds two police cars came to a screeching halt at the end of the driveway. One of the officers ran after the fleeing Marcos, while the other one entered the garage with his weapon drawn. Tracy was relieved to see it was Officer Foreman, with whom she had often worked. She pointed to the figure still writhing on the ground.

"Well, you did a good job, Tracy. This man probably won't spawn any little thieves."

"And this one has a broken nose," the other officer said, bringing a handcuffed but struggling Marcos into the garage. "Do you know these guys?"

" Don't know who they are. They don't live in this area, but I've seen them on several occasions. I think they've been following me around town."

After the intruders were secured in the back of the cruisers, Tracy filled the officers in on her two encounters with the two thugs. "They asked where the old guy's stuff was. I'm not sure what they are after. I assume they meant Mr. Levine. There's nothing of great value among his possessions, except a desk, which isn't even here. Even if it had been, I don't see their car on the street. It would look pretty obvious, them carrying *that* down the street in the middle of the night. I don't think even they are dumb enough to try that." Tracy suddenly remembered, "By the way, I filed an accident report the other day. Could you tell Officer Henry I found out who was in the other car?" She shot an accusing glare at Jack.

"Well, we'll find out what this is all about once we get them down to the station. It was a good thing for them you had your alarm on, otherwise they might not have survived their mission, whatever it was," Officer Foreman laughed. "We'll check around back and make sure everything is locked up tight. These guys won't be back tonight, or any other time if they know what's good for them."

At least she found out why the guys were following her, but that raised more questions. *What was in those meager possessions that they wanted and why? Were they looking for a specific thing, or just hoping to sell what they could find?* She wasn't sure they had seen the desk, or if they would even know it's value. Nothing there was worth all the attention. Did they act alone or did someone put them up to this? And what about the old gentleman who kept turning up? *There's something missing here. What am I overlooking?*

Chapter Five

The phone rang and Tracy quickly picked it up, thinking the police might have news about the break-in.

"Hi there, anything new happen while I was gone?" Jean asked.

"I am so glad you're back. I desperately need some answers and you are the only one who can provide them."

"I see I was missed," Jean laughed. "What's happened?"

Tracy told her about the break-in and the old man. "I don't know what all these people are after." Tracy breathed a frustrated sigh. "It's a mystery to me. I know greed brings people out of the woodwork when someone passes away, but this has me stumped. I'm hoping there's something in the diary that will shed some light on everything. I need to find the daughter, too, and get this whole mess settled. Soon."

"How about after my classes this afternoon? We can have dinner at your place and go over it, or better yet, mine. That way we won't have any interruptions, given all the interest in your place."

"I think you're right. Can I bring anything?"

"Would you mind stopping by the market and picking up some veggies for salad? I don't have any of that stuff here, but I'll pull something out of the freezer for the main course. See you tonight, say around six?"

"I'll be there. Thanks, Jean, you don't know how much I appreciate your help."

"What are friends for? Just be careful."

Tracy hung up the phone and finished dressing. She wanted to go by the gym to get in some kickboxing practice if she did nothing else today. That would help get the kinks out from last night's debacle.

Later a stop by the market, pick up the diary from the bank vault, and then meet Jean at her house.

"Hey, long time no see." Clyde gave Tracy a good-natured slap on her shoulder as she dropped her bag in the locker. "You know the tournament is fast approaching and we need to do some work on a few of your kicks."

"Sorry, Clyde, some things came up that have kept me pretty busy." Tracy spared him the details of her work, but gave him a blow-by-blow description of her fight last night.

"See, this is important. Your lessons probably saved your life. I wish I could have been there and seen the look on those fellows' faces," Clyde laughed. "Let's get busy and catch you up on your instructions."

Clyde watched Tracy stretch and do her warm-up exercises before putting her through the different routines. Several times he stopped her and said, "Concentrate. You aren't concentrating, Tracy. You didn't leave everything at the door when you came in. Now, watch. Do like this." Clyde led her through the different forms, re-positioning her when she got off balance. He then let her finish on her own.

The hour flew by. Tracy retrieved her bag and headed for the showers. She definitely suffered the effects of staying away from her routine longer than usual, but she felt good about her lessons today.

"See you back here tomorrow?"

"Hopefully. I can't promise, but I sure intend to try."

Tracy tossed her bag into the back seat and was about to get into her car when she noticed a large black sedan parked a few spaces down the street. Almost sure this was the car that had been following her, she closed the door and started walking toward it. Suddenly, the engine roared to life and the car whipped into traffic. Brakes squealed as drivers tried to avoid him. When the car sped by she caught a glimpse of the white haired man behind the wheel.

Mentally making a note of the license plate number, Tracy got into her car and searched in her purse for something to write on. She would never catch up to him now without risking an accident, but her friend in the police department could deal with him. She had frightened him off and still no answers. For the time being she had to be satisfied.

Later, Tracy rang Jean's doorbell and cautiously glanced around the street, making sure she was not followed. The young men were still in jail, but the older man seemed to be everywhere. Whatever his reason for following her, she certainly didn't want to involve her friend in her problems any more than she could help.

"Hey, girl, come on in this house." There was a trace of laughter in Jean's voice. She grabbed Tracy and gave her a big hug. "Have you been assaulting any more of our citizens?" She closed the door and led Tracy down the hall. In the kitchen, Jean took the groceries and set them on the counter.

"Seriously, Trace, I wish you would hire yourself a bodyguard until this mess is over. I worry about you living there all by yourself with all this going on."

"And who do you have living with you these days?"

"Don't change the subject. You know I don't have people following me and trying to break into my house."

" 'Trying to', are the key words here. What a bunch of losers! I wouldn't send them to take out my trash, they're so incompetent."

"How do you know their replacement will be incompetent, too?"

"What makes you think there will be?" Tracy scooted on to a barstool. "I need to get this diary translated and find out just what everyone is after."

"What makes you think there won't?" Pausing, Jean glanced at her friend but didn't give her a chance to answer. "Well, let's get dinner on the table and we can get started. I have the steaks almost done and the potatoes are being microwaved. Once the salad is made we should be able to eat. This would be the veggies for it, right?" Jean asked, shaking the plastic bag she took from Tracy.

"Yep; and dessert. I picked up some frozen yogurt and brownies."

"You didn't."

"Yes, I did. We'll just drink lots of water and that will dilute the calories." She grinned at Jean. "Like you have to worry about that anyway." As long as Tracy had known Jean, her friend had always been slender and never bothered about her weight. Tracy, on the other hand, had to be vigilant because she put the pounds on easily.

Both had such busy schedules lately that it had been a couple of months since they had really talked. So, all through dinner the two women talked about mutual friends with whom one or the other had lost contact and about Jean's work.

Jean was unhappy with her job again and was thinking about moving away. It wasn't the first time she mentioned re-locating, but this time she seemed more determined. Even though the thought saddened Tracy, she showed no sign of it to her friend, but rather listened to her unload the stress. Usually she was okay once she got everything out in the open and had someone to help her look at the pros and cons. Hopefully, this would work again. But there was something different this time.

"You're holding out on me. You're talking to someone who knows you all too well. What's really wrong?"

Jean pushed her food around on the plate and seemed to be struggling inwardly. "You know how I always wanted kids and Norman didn't? Well, he and the woman who he left me for have two children and she is pregnant again." Jean's eyes brimmed with tears as she stared at her plate.

"What a son-of-a bitch." Tracy reached across the table and put her hand on Jean's. "I'm sorry, not about the son-of-a-bitch part, but because he continues to hurt you. How did you find out?"

"I ran into one of the professors who works at his college while I was on this latest sabbatical. "

"And that person was all too eager to give you the latest."

"I'm not sure what her intentions were."

"Well, I bet I know. Say, isn't he a little old to be having a new baby?"

"He is, but she's not. She's fifteen years younger." Jean cast her eyes downward.

"Oh yeah, I forgot. She was jail bait when he met her."

"They don't say that anymore." Jean offered a tear stained laugh. "Besides, she was nineteen."

"What don't they say anymore?"

"Jail-bait. It's an old-fashioned term."

"I'm an old-fashioned girl. Michael keeps trying to get me to move into the electronic age. Anyway, that's how I see it. Jail-bait, even at nineteen." Tracy watched Jean's expression and asked, "Is this why you want to change jobs? To get far away from him?"

Jean cast her eyes downward and changed the subject. "Okay, that's the end of my sad tale. It's all so insignificant compared to what our Mr. Levine went through. Bring out the journal and let's get started." Jean pushed her chair back and began clearing the table. When Tracy followed her lead she stopped her. "I'll do this. I'm just going to put them in the sink for now. It won't take but a minute to load them in the dishwasher later. Mr. Levine awaits our rescue."

1938— Nearing Hanukkah

I discovered an abandoned farmhouse the other night on my way to the village and we are now staying in it. Hopefully, we can stay through the winter. Sadly, the medicine came too late for the sick boy and we lost him. I think it was pneumonia. There are altogether three families with a total of four children and myself, along with Josef. (His family was murdered during the raid of Kristallnacht while he was away on business)

The mood is a somber one, especially with Hanukkah approaching and all of us remembering how it was in past years, celebrating with family and friends in our own place. But we must make the most of it; we are still free and we are working diligently to make the farmhouse more habitable and warm.

It seems ages since I put Esther and Hannah on the train. I sure miss them and would like to have them here with me right now. I'm cold and lonely even with these wonderful people nearby who are in the same situation as me, trying desperately to get out before it's too late. I wonder if I did the right thing letting them go. Maybe they would be safer with me and at least I would know what's happening to them. Stop it, Sam; you're tougher than this, as tough as they are and as tough as you need to be. You must survive and meet with Esther and Hannah as planned.

1939, January—

Not a very happy New Year so far, although I guess I should be thankful just for surviving this long, many have not. Winter has been long and hard so far, and thankfully we had shelter most of the coldest part of it. We have traveled only about 139 kilometers since I left home and met up with my new friends. Not very far, but we've had to stay off the main roads for fear of being stopped and searched and having our things stolen from us. Those who resist can be killed. I'm a fugitive in my own country without even committing a crime. How dispiriting!

German soldiers are everywhere and well armed. More and more they murder my people, as I have seen with my very own eyes. A family was pulled from their automobile this very day and shot dead alongside the roadway. Who should have been the murderer but my new nemesis, Karl Mueller! I think he may have been looking for me. My stomach turned and rejected the meager breakfast I had earlier.

The farmhouse where we have been staying is near Leipzig. Josef and I went into town, skirting around the main part of the city. We needed supplies and petrol, which is getting harder and harder to find.

Josef and I went into town around dusk. Approaching town we saw a contingent of soldiers who look as though they were just loafing and killing time. We avoided directly crossing their path but did not attempt to sneak around, knowing that type of behavior would only raise suspicions. Josef suggested that he buy the petrol while I shopped for the groceries and other needs.

I went into the store and left Josef to find the fuel. About half way through my shopping, looking out the window, I saw him talking to the Captain of the German patrol. This was not good. I needed to find out what was being said. I told the clerk I needed to check with my wife about other items and asked if he would hold my purchases until I returned. Outside, I went about half a block to a narrow street meant only for pedestrians and bicycles. I walked a short distance back toward the main road where the German officer was talking to Josef and stayed next to the building in the shadows and then hid under a stairwell. I could hear them but they could not see me. I listened for a few minutes, not long, but long enough to know we were in trouble. He told them of my entries in what he called a log, where we had been, whom we had seen and where we were staying. I have no idea what he hoped to gain. I hurried back to the store and finished my shopping, all the while working on a plan.

When I left the store Josef was waiting for me as though nothing had happened. We walked to the edge of town and put the can of petrol and supplies into my old Mercedes and climbed in. Well out of town now and still a ways from the farmhouse we came to a stand of trees on both sides of the road. I pulled over and stopped the car, telling Joseph I needed to go into the woods for a moment. As I returned to the car he was leaning against the fender smoking a cigarette. I slammed the large rock I had collected from the woods against the side of his head. He dropped like his legs were suddenly pulled out from under him. After making sure he was dead I pulled him into the woods and covered him with leaves weighted down with some branches.

" Holy moly!" Jean exclaimed, "He's a murderer."

"I wonder if that has anything to do with the old fellow who suddenly showed up with an interest in our Samuel? Maybe he was a relative of this Josef and when he read about Samuel's death in the German newspapers he wanted to make sure it was the same Samuel Levine?" Tracy went to the cabinet and pulled out two wine glasses. "Read on while I pour us a glass of wine. I definitely feel the need for one right now."

After wiping my hands with some damp leaves I checked myself over in front of the headlights. I looked fine but I had to get my nerves under control before reaching the others. Josef had tried to find favor with the Germans by telling them about us and where we were going and they wanted him to find out who was helping the Jews. He told them he would call in a couple of days with a report on our whereabouts and the other information they wanted. They would not expect to hear from him for a few days, so we would be okay for now. Josef had put us all in jeopardy and had to be silenced. I will tell the others he just decided to go on alone. I can't remember if I told Josef the name of the family in Lyon where I was headed. If he knew that information, had he given it to the Germans? I must step up my journey and get to Lyon as soon as possible.

1939, February—

Journey has been so bone weary and dangerous I have not been able to write anything. Now, we have finally made it to Lyon, but too late. It took me days to find my contact, as they had moved out ahead of a raid. A raid, I suspect, is to be credited to Josef. My poor dearest Esther has died and is buried in Lyon, France.

When news of the impending raid came, my daughter was taken by a family named Steinfeld and is on her way to America with them. My contact has given me back the letters I sent, as well as the address in America where the Steinfelds live. Alas, my wife and daughter never knew I had written to them because the mail was so slow getting here. They thought I was dead because of all the terrible news coming out of Germany. I don't know if I have the strength or desire to go on.

"How awful," Tracy moaned. She got up from the table and poured more wine in Jean's glass, then topped off hers. She wiped tears from her eyes with the corner of her napkin. "How does one go on after all that? For the life of me, I can't understand how one human being like Hitler can inflict so much pain and death on another and then get other people to do the same. I'll *never* be able to understand it."

Jean nodded in agreement. She was too moved by the journal to speak for a few minutes. "So, that Josef probably did tell the Germans about Mr. Levine's contact," she mused, her voice sounding tired. "How else would they know?"

"Do you want to finish this another time?" Tracy asked her friend, suddenly realizing how late it was.

"I am kinda tired. Why don't you crash here tonight? We can get an early start in the morning. Saturday is always quiet around here."

"Great idea since I wasn't planning to drive after all the wine I've consumed," Tracy answered. "I don't want to tie up your weekend, though."

Jean quirked one eyebrow and grinned. "I checked my calendar and fortunately I have the morning open. I also have the middle of the day, the afternoon and the evening open. My life is not filled with the excitement that colors yours." She went into the other room and returned with a nightgown. "You know your way around, but if you can't find something just holler."

The next morning Tracy stumbled into the kitchen, trying to focus her vision. The aroma of bacon cooking and coffee perking summoned her from the back bedroom before she had a chance to brush away the cobwebs of sleep. Not only that, but the night had held many disjointed dreams. She was having trouble overcoming the weariness caused by her restless sleep.

"Well, look at you, Miss Suzy Homemaker. What time is it and how long have you been up?"

"It's seven-thirty and I have been up since six— the usual time I get up." Jean removed the pan from the stove and scooped out the bacon with a fork, placing it on a paper towel to drain. "How did you sleep?"

"I ran from Germans most of the night and fought my way through weird dreams. Guess that's what I get for drinking two glasses of wine."

"Well, if you're like me you never sleep very well in a strange bed."

Tracy waggled her eyebrows and said, "It depends on who's in there with me."

Jean laughed and slapped her friend on the shoulder. "Speaking of Michael, when are you seeing him again?"

"When this is all over and I can go away with a clear mind. Michael deserves my full attention; something I'm ashamed to say I haven't been able to give him lately. I also want to be able to have a good time when I go out there and not worry about anything here."

"Well, let's see if we can't get started toward that end. We'll eat, then bring out the journal and see what's happening."

1939, February—

Days have passed and I must be moving on. I can't stay with these people forever and put them at further risk. I am a wanted man. The Picards, who are my contacts, are arranging to send me to Shanghai, where I have been told, a visa is not required. Once there I can get papers to go to America and try to find my daughter.

1939, March 1—

Arrived in Shanghai after about four weeks at sea. Nothing but bombed-out buildings that I can see. So different from anything I could imagine. I will wait until dark to leave the ship when it is safer as I was warned the bridge is heavily guarded and to be careful of the barbed wire.

1939, March 6—

I will never forget the horrors of this place. It is occupied by the Japanese, friends of the Nazis. But worse are the conditions here. Stench of decay and food of every nation cooking on the streets, and early every morning Chinese men called "coolies" go around the city collecting the dead.

Shanghai is crime ridden. There are opium dens and kidnapping is a common occurrence. Multitudes of pick-pockets, beggars and prostitutes haunt the streets. Typhoons flood the city and mosquitoes bring malaria. It is hot here and the mosquito netting around my makeshift bed blocks what little air I get in the one room apartment I share with three other fellows. It is difficult to breathe. Much of the time windows are left open, making our belongings easy prey to thieves. I learned from a man who has been here for a few months to hide my possessions well, for thieves not only pillage in the daytime when folks are away, they even strike while people sleep. I keep my journal under my pillow and inside my shirt in the daytime. Not that they would steal it but I don't want to take the chance. I am keeping this for my daughter.

1939, April—

Working at anything I can find, which isn't much, to earn money. So many like me trying to survive in these slums, plus there are the coolies working for far less. Sold some belongings, too, to get enough money for documents.

1939, April 30—

One of my roommates became so desperate he tried begging and has disappeared. Racketeer leaders control the streets and I fear they are responsible for his disappearance. One does not interfere in another's territory on these mean streets.

1939, May 2—

No time to write. I have arranged to work on a ship headed out of Shanghai for England. From there I will be able to book passage to Cuba. Am told that is the easiest way to get to America. I am glad to be leaving. So many here in desperate situation and the danger is great. . .

1939, Late June—

I've heard we are the second ship to be turned away from Cuba. Too many refugees already there and Cuba's situation allows no more. We have sailed to several ports and been denied admission. People have lost all hope and there have been reports of people taking their own lives. Others tried, but thankfully did not succeed.

1939, July—

Finally, appeals made to the president of America have allowed us to dock in New York. There is much jubilation among those still able to celebrate. At last I am on my way to my dear Hannah. . .

1939, August—

Stowed away in train container and on my way. Arriving in Rapid City, South Dakota, I find the family has taken Hannah and moved, leaving no forwarding address. In talking to neighbors, I discover they have moved to a town in Northern California. I will find a job here to finance my journey there.

1940, January—

It is bitter cold in this town and I am happy to be leaving. It took me longer than expected to earn the needed money. I understand California is a much warmer climate and I think I'm going to like that.

1940, March, California—

I have searched for weeks up and down the coast and can find no trace of the family. I have made advertisements in the paper even as far away as San Diego and will wait to hear. So far nothing. . .

"The next few pages are blank. Nothing about all the years after that, where he was or what he did until he came here. There is just this entry made last year which is addressed to Hannah."

2007, April—

My Dearest Hannah,

I am at the end of my life's journey and I have been unsuccessful at finding you. Hopefully, in my death, this journal will reach you or your family. Please read it from cover to cover. It will answer all your questions and help you rediscover your heritage, a valuable asset for your future and that of your family, if you have one. I wonder, as I have all these years, what kind of person you became. Am I a grandfather? Do your children know of me? Do you even remember me? How very much I have missed you.

"And the last entry, which reads:"

My darling daughter,
I share with you some thoughts I've gained through the years:
Treasure love but do not love treasure.
Much of the first and some of the second
Are the best measure.
Love will bind you to him and him to you
But too many riches will bind you both in chains
And together not long will you remain.
Yea, empty pockets breed contempt
And few of us are exempt
From holding those we love to blame
When with so little we strive in vain.
So riches, some are welcome indeed
As we want to fill our daily need.
To understand a man you must go inside
For it is there the mysteries lie.
Beneath the covers one must look
For each of us is like a book.
The jewels of knowledge abound inside
For it is here that truth resides.
And with each reading more is revealed
Until finally we know what's real.'

"Well, I feel a little let down now that we have finished his journal. I will miss living those moments with him," Jean sniffed, wiping away a tear. " He went through so much. How sad for that family, though, that they never hooked up again."

"This part is a little cryptic. What do you suppose it means? And who is this Mueller fellow he mentions in the beginning. Why was he after Samuel?"

A loud crash from the front of the house interrupted the conversation, bringing the two women to their feet.

"Stay here while I go investigate."

"No way, I'm coming with you and I'm bringing the phone in case we have to call the cops. After all, I missed the last time you whupped up on someone."

Outside, a large black sedan had plowed into a parked vehicle and, as Tracy got to the car, she noticed the driver slumped over the wheel.

"Call 911, Jean," Tracy yelled to her friend, who had yet to reach the accident. "I think my little old man has really done it this time." Not wanting to inflict further damage, Tracy carefully checked to see if the man was breathing. As far as she could tell he was still alive, but there was a lot of blood where he hit the windshield.

The sound of sirens filled the air as the paramedic ambulance rounded the corner. Tracy moved out of the paramedics' way and let them go about their business. After they removed the injured man, Tracy asked if he was going to be all right.

"Don't know yet, Miss. Are you related?"

"No, but I am somewhat acquainted with him."

The paramedic gave her a puzzled look, but before he could ask what she meant, he was called away by his partner. They loaded the stretcher into the ambulance and one man climbed into the back while the other jumped in front, quickly pulling away and reactivating the siren.

"You think he'll make it?" Jean asked, gazing after the departing ambulance.

"I don't know. It looked pretty serious. I think I'll go down to the hospital and make sure." Tracy stood a moment looking at the sedan while the officers started their investigation. She saw nothing in there that would tell her why the man had been following her, so she went back inside to get dressed.

On the way to the hospital, more questions filled Tracy's mind. *Was he related to Mr. Levine? If that was the case, why hadn't he come forward and said so? Or was he connected someway with the man Samuel had killed so long ago? What was he looking for? Was he even going to make it after the accident?*

Chapter Six

Tracy idly thumbed through the months' old edition of the Time magazine she found on the table. Hospital waiting rooms always made her depressed and she tried to keep her mind elsewhere, but without much success. Every time someone approached she glanced up, hoping it would be the doctor. She wasn't certain he would give her any information but since there was no one else here on the patient's behalf, she hoped he would talk to her.

"Miss Chapman?"

"Yes, over here," Tracy answered. She put the magazine down and met the doctor in the middle of the room.

"Are you Mr. Dietrick's granddaughter?" The doctor pulled the green cap from his head and ran his long slender fingers through his silver hair. Perspiration stained dark circles reaching half way up the cap and around the neck of his hospital scrub top.

"No, but I was hopeful you could tell me about his condition anyway." Not wanting to take up too much of the doctor's time, Tracy explained her situation as briefly as possible. "I was thinking he might tell me why he's been following me and if he knows anything about the whereabouts of Mr. Levine's family."

"It may be a while before you can talk to him. I'm afraid he cracked his head a pretty good one and is still unconscious. With head injuries you just never know about the outcome and Mr. Dietrick, being an elderly person— well, it's just too soon to say."

"His name is Dietrick?" The doctor was hesitant about answering and Tracy offered, "I can give you personal references from the police department and from the medical examiner's office with whom I work closely. I assure you I have no criminal intentions."

"Yes, it's Rutger Dietrick, according to his driver's license."

"Then he lives in the United States?" Tracy was puzzled since she was sure this was the man who called her shop and spoke with a heavy German accent. If he were from another country he wouldn't have a drivers license.

The doctor shook his head, "It's an international driver's license. I'm afraid I can't give you any more information at this time. I need to get into O.R., so if you'll excuse me."

Did Dietrick find out about Mr. Levine's death from the local papers, or from Germany? She was certain the obituary was not published in any other state because, at the time of his death, there was nothing to indicate Samuel had lived anywhere other than Germany and California. *So, if it was Germany, then why did he rush over here so quickly and then not get in touch with the authorities?* One more puzzle for Tracy to solve. She really needed to talk to the old man.

"One more thing, Doctor. Would it be all right if I stop in from time to time and check on Mr. Dietrick?"

"It depends on his condition. When and if he regains consciousness, I don't think he will be up to interrogations."

"I promise I will abide by your instructions. Right now I just want him to recover as much as you do." The doctor raised an eyebrow and she continued, "Not just because I need answers, either. I feel bad for him being hurt and all."

"You might as well go on home for now. He is in the Intensive Care Unit and you won't be able to see him until he has been moved to a room." The doctor turned to leave, then added, "That is, if he wants visitors."

"Thanks, Doctor, I appreciate your time."

Another day had passed since the accident and Tracy checked with the hospital. Just before noon the nurse informed her they would be moving Dietrick into a private room and she could come and visit as long as she didn't tire or upset him.

On her way to the hospital, Tracy stopped by the florist and bought a colorful bouquet of flowers. He still wasn't strong or recovered enough for her to ask him questions. Perhaps, if she visited often though, he might feel comfortable with her presence and answer questions when he was able.

Tracy stood awkwardly in the doorway, flowers in hand, waiting for the nurse to remove the luncheon tray from Dietrick's bed. She glanced at Tracy and said to her patient, "I believe there is a young lady here to see you. Shall I raise your head a little so you can visit?"

Mr. Dietrick looked so small lying there, head bandaged and a tube delivering some sort of medication through his arm. He blinked as if to clear his vision, his eyes appearing very large behind the wire rim eyeglasses. He looked puzzled. Then suddenly recognizing her, he quickly shifted in his bed and turned his head away.

The nurse took the flowers from Tracy and went to look for a vase. Dietrick looked to see if it was Tracy who left the room, then turned away again. She went around the bed and faced him.

"Mr. Dietrick, I'm only here to make sure you are all right and see if you need anything."

"Why?" he asked feebly.

"Do you have anyone in town to see to your needs?"

"Nein," he answered, eyeing her suspiciously.

"Then, there you go. Being all alone is no fun and especially if you are in a hospital— " Tracy glanced around the room. Seeing a chair against the far wall, she dragged it close to the bed. "Do you mind if I come to visit until you get better? I promise I will leave anytime you feel uncomfortable."

Mr. Dietrick shrugged, his gaze suddenly fixed on the sheet covering him. He appeared to be very uncomfortable, and Tracy decided to conclude her visit for now. She returned the chair and came back to the bed.

"I'll go now and let you get some rest. If you need anything let me know. I'll leave my phone number with the nurse and check in on you in a day or so." She waited to see if he would answer, but he simply stared at the ceiling.

Tracy kicked off her shoes at the door and put her keys and mail on the table. Feeling a little down over the failures of the day, she went to the freezer and pulled out a carton of Ben and Jerry's Cherry Garcia ice cream and a spoon from the cabinet drawer. Not bothering to get a bowl, she plunged the spoon into the frozen delicacy and began to eat. It might not help matters, but it sure did taste good.

Not only were there no answers in the journal, other than what happened to Mr. Levine over the years, but Dietrick also gave no hint at how he figured in all this mess. Her one hope regarding Dietrick's background was in the abilities of a private detective she used occasionally; she decided to give him a call.

T. Nicholas Greger, Nick to his friends, was the best as far as Tracy was concerned. No one knew what the 'T' stood for and they had long since quit trying to find out. Besides being the best, he made her laugh, which was very important to Tracy. Even now, her smile turned to a chuckle as his image sprang vividly to mind.

Nick always looked as though he had just gotten out of bed. His light brown hair, sprinkled with flecks of grey, stood on end and a stubble of whiskers camouflaged a blemished complexion. Broad shoulders only tapered slightly to a generous waist, thickened by too many surveillances and desk duties. But his charm was in his sense of humor and easy manner. He was true to his word and said it like it was; No "pussyfootin' around". He was not pretentious nor did he accept "snootiness" from anyone else.

"Hi, Nick. Got a favor to ask." Tracy told him briefly about her case. "His full name is Rutger Dietrick. I need to know what role he plays in all this as soon as possible. There is another man, too, a Karl Mueller, who Samuel mentions in his diary. He may have hired this guy, Dietrick. I don't know much about him, though, except that Mr. Levine considered Mueller a threat at one time in his life. Can you help me, or are you bogged down with cases?"

"I wish." Nick heaved a sigh on the other end of the line. "This computer age has really cut down on my work load, at least the finding missing persons part of it."

"Rutger Dietrick may have been already been here in the States because he arrived in Monet Cove pretty quickly. I'm not sure if that is temporary or not, his being in the States. That's neither here nor there, at least at this point. The information I want will probably be in Germany, I think, and unfortunately I don't have the time."

"So you think the other man might be involved, too?"

"Well, I wanted to keep an open mind, but I guess we'll find out eventually. That's all the information I have at the moment. Hopefully it will give you a good enough start. " She felt a sense of relief, knowing that if there was any information at all, Nick would find it. That would be one worry off her mind.

"I'll get right on it Tracy."

The sound of someone fiddling with the door lock interrupted the conversation. She wasn't sure if the person actually had a key, or if a tool was being used to force their way in. Placing the phone on its stand, she glanced around the room looking for something handy to use as a weapon, her heart racing. Finding nothing, she walked across the room so she would be behind the door when it was opened. Once in place, she turned just as the person entered. Already in self-defense mode, she almost sent a roundhouse kick in the direction of the intruder.

"Whoa, wait a minute, Tracy!" Michael cautioned.

"What? Michael! What are you doing here?"

"Didn't you get my message? I called this morning and left a message that I would be here this afternoon. I figured you'd be busy, so I took the shuttle down from the airport and grabbed a cab here."

"I'm so sorry," Tracy said, wrapping her arms around him and giving him a big hug. "I've been at the hospital— "

"What's wrong? What happened?" Michael asked anxiously, pushing her at arm's length and visually checking her out from head to toe.

Tracy explained about Dietrick and the car crash. "And to what do I owe this unexpected surprise?"

" I was in the neighborhood and decided to stop by."

"Liar," Tracy chuckled. "What really brought you out this way?"

"No, really, I had some business in San Francisco and since I was so close I decided to stop by," Michael insisted. "Besides, I've been worried and wanted to make sure you were all right and protecting yourself. I know you and figured you'd be right in the thick of things. I was going to surprise you but decided at the last moment that I had better let you know I was on my way, what with all the mysterious things happening in your life."

Tracy laughed, "Thanks for the thought anyway. I just haven't gotten around to checking my messages." She hugged him again, enjoying the warmth of his body next to hers. She had to admit she was glad he had come. "Umm, you feel good and I hate to let you go."

"Then don't. I kinda like this arrangement."

" First things first. You must be pretty tired and hungry from your long trip. I can order some take-out while you get comfortable. I'm sorta hungry myself. The little bit of ice cream just now wasn't filling enough."

Michael tipped the carton so he could see the label. "Hitting the Cherry Garcia again?" His mouth twitched with amusement. "Things must not be going along so smoothly, huh?"

"Ah, you know me too well, my love." Tracy went to the kitchen and pulled out some papers that were clipped together inside a drawer. "You want Pizza, Chinese or Mexican?"

"I think Mexican, if you don't mind," Michael called from the bedroom where he had just deposited his duffel bag. "You got a place in mind?"

"You bet and they deliver. When you come back in here you can make a selection from the menu. I already know what I want."

After dinner was ordered, Tracy set up the table on her deck while Michael took a quick shower. She lit the candle a third time and quickly replaced the large glass globe over the flame before the breeze could blow it out again. Pouring two tall glasses of lemonade, she set them on a tray, along with some silverware and napkins. As she carried the tray outside, her neighbor waved from the beach.

"Hi there, Cole, how's it going?" Tracy called.

"Hi, Tracy. I've been meaning to come over and talk to you ever since I got back into town." He leaned down and scratched Beau on the head. When he rose up again he noticed she was setting the table. "Oh, I see you're about to eat. Sorry. I just wanted to tell you that the last time I ran down the beach— it was after dark a few days ago, maybe.

"Anyway, I almost ran over some dude all dressed in dark clothing. He was with another guy and they seemed disturbed when I ran up on them. I think they might have been casing the neighborhood. It would probably be a good idea to be extra careful and keep your doors locked."

"What's this about locking your doors?" Michael asked. "Something else going on you haven't told me about?"

"Oh, sorry, Tracy, I didn't know you had company," Cole apologized awkwardly.

"It's okay," Tracy assured him, "Cole, this is Michael, a dear friend. Michael, this is Cole Sanders and his beautiful Dalmatian, Beau. They are my neighbors from down the beach."

"Pleasure to meet the both of you. Tracy has mentioned you before." Michael leaned on the railing, looking down at the two. "He is a beautiful dog. Bet he's a great friend, too." "Pleased to meet you, too, Michael. Thanks, and he is my best buddy. Well, I don't want to interrupt anymore so I'll just finish my run with Beau. Hope to see you again, Michael." And with that he jogged down the beach, the dog running just ahead of him.

"Sorry, I didn't mean to chase him off," Michael said, brushing back a lock of damp hair. "What was he talking about when I came out?"

"Oh, that. Just that he has seen suspicious people around and he wanted me to be careful."

"Okay, Trace, out with it. I can always tell when you are covering up something."

"Really, Michael, it was nothing."

Michael pulled his chair out and sat down stretching his long legs ahead of him. "I want to know the whole story."

"Saved by the bell." Tracy gave an exaggerated sigh when the doorbell chimed. "Dinner has arrived." She quickly ran downstairs to the front door, relieved at the momentary reprieve. It would give her time to get her thoughts together and decide how much she wanted to tell Michael about the incident with the two hoodlums. As they ate their dinner, Tracy told him about the two men who had broken into her house, leaving out her battle with them. "Fortunately, the alarm was working and the police came and hauled them away."

"What do you suppose they were after?" Michael asked, watching her reaction closely.

"I really don't know." She avoided his eyes, staring down at her plate. "Probably looking for something to steal and sell for drugs. There is a lot of that going on."

"But you don't really think that was the case?" Michael frowned, his eyes level under drawn brows.

"No, I guess not," she relented. "I think it had something to do with Mr. Levine and or Mr. Dietrick. I haven't heard anything from the police, so I don't suppose the two young men are talking to them yet."

"Are you leaving anything out that I should know?"

"No, I guess that's it."

Michael's eyebrow shot up. He folded his arms across his chest and waited.

"Well, maybe there was a little roughing up."

"You or them?"

"Michael, oh ye of little faith."

Michael threw his head back and let out a great peal of laughter. "My money was on you, I know what you are capable of. That's how I knew there was more to this story than you were telling." Suddenly his expression stilled and he grew serious, "I wish you would be more careful though, Trace. One of these days you aren't going to be so lucky."

"Luck had nothing to do with it, Michael. I have trained hard and long to be able to defend myself." Annoyance colored her tone.

"Maybe 'luck' wasn't the right word to use. One of these days you might not be able to defend yourself. People are killed everyday, some trained even better than you. Cops for instance."

"Let's talk about something else. Tell me what you've been doing and how much you missed me." She grinned mischievously and waggled her eyebrows.

Michael stared out at the sea. The red sun was sinking into the ocean and the damp air felt suddenly chilly. He knew the serious conversation was over and his brow furrowed deeply with concern. For a moment, the only sound was the breaking waves upon the beach. Suddenly he shivered, feeling the dampness enveloping him. It seemed to seep into his very soul.

"Let's go in, it's getting cold." He began clearing the table and Tracy followed his lead. Silently, they shared the task of cleaning up the kitchen, each occupied with thoughts about their discussion. Michael rarely voiced his concern over her work even though it was uppermost in his thoughts. This was one time he wasn't going to hold back.

"Michael, please don't worry." Tracy broke the silence first. "Those guys have been arrested and now are known by the police. They wouldn't dare try anything else. And Mr. Dietrick is an old and feeble man, not able to cause me any physical harm."

"Is he the one who hired those jerks? What keeps him from hiring someone else?"

"I don't know if he did. I haven't had a chance to really talk to him. They could've been acting on their own as far as that goes. I thought at first those guys wanted retaliation because I insulted them, but they mentioned Mr. Levine's stuff," Tracy said, trying to put all the pieces together. "The obituary was printed in the newspaper along with his address. Maybe they went in to take whatever they could find of value. When they found the apartment empty and, having seen me there, assumed correctly that I had removed his things."

"How much longer do you think this is going to take?"

"Dunno, but I have a friend helping so it should be soon. He needs to have a burial as quickly as possible— Jewish tradition."

"Well, it can't be soon enough for me." A muscle quivered at his jaw. He gripped her shoulders and looked directly into her eyes. "I want you out of this before something bad happens."

"Let's not spoil the evening with an argument." Tracy tiptoed and placed a long kiss on his mouth, then drew back and studied his face. She changed the subject. "Now, tell me about your business trip. What are you up to now?" She really did want to know what was going on in his life and, hopefully, this would get his mind off the mess in which she was involved.

Michael knew it was fruitless to pursue the subject any further. He sat down at the table and leaned on his forearms. He could see Tracy was relieved to change the subject. And he was anxious to tell her about his good luck, but he wasn't going to give up his objections to her case.

"Remember I was telling you about a deal I was working on? Well, I think it is actually coming to fruition." Michael's eyes danced with excitement as he explained his new venture to Tracy. "I've decided to market my cattle directly to the retailer, and today I had a meeting with the management of Green Bean Markets in San Francisco."

"Why would you change the way you sell your cattle?" Tracy asked, "I thought everything was going well the way it was."

"It is going well, very well, actually. Over the past few years cattle prices have been very strong and I've managed to put some money away for when the prices drop, which they will, they always do. The cattle business runs in cycles."

"So-o-o, if things are going well, what do you expect to gain by going direct to the retailer?" Tracy interrupted.

"Well, I raise my cattle without the use of added hormones or growth implants and with minimal use of antibiotics."

"You're losing me here. Why would you need to add hormones and what do you mean by minimal use of antibiotics?"

"Most ranchers add hormones in the form of an implant that is attached to the ear and is, in effect, a time-release method of giving the animal additional hormones. The economic basis for doing this is that the implant increases the conversion rate of whatever animal they are used on."

"Conversion rate?"

"It means that for a given amount of feed ration the animal will convert more of that ration into muscle and fat. The economic benefit being that the cattle will gain weight faster and spend less time in the feedlot before reaching market weight."

"And what do you do differently?"

"I have a small feed yard on my property and I feed my own cattle. You saw it when you were out there," Michael reminded Tracy. "I don't want to implant them. I have to feed my cattle about forty-five days longer for them to reach market weight. When I sell them to the packers, I'll get a little more based on a higher percentage of choice and prime, which will happen when cattle are allowed to mature naturally." Michael studied her thoughtfully before continuing, making sure he wasn't losing her. "But it's not enough to offset the time on feed for my cattle. Remember, I have to feed my cattle about a month and a half longer and they eat around twenty-five pounds each day. So you can see why ranchers are inclined to use implants."

"But what does it do to the people who eat the meat from those implanted cattle?"

"I don't want to imply that the beef you or anyone else buys at the supermarket is in any way unsafe. The USDA—United States Department of Agriculture— doesn't allow growth implants sixty days prior to processing, and the USDA performs tests for remaining residue. That assures that no unsafe levels of the added growth promotants remain in the beef."

"So by going direct to the retailer you expect to get enough additional money for your cattle to cover the cost of raising them the natural way?"

"You got it. I think the Green Bean stores are just the ones who may see the benefit of having a naturally raised branded beef program. The twenty-five stores they have are small enough for me to supply, but large enough to take all the cattle I raise each year. And from what I read, the smaller progressive chains of stores are always looking for ways to set themselves apart from the really big guys."

"Tell me a little bit about the antibiotic issue."

"A lot of antibiotics are given to the cattle, as well as other animals, as a preventative measure and not just for a specific disease. Antibiotics are administered both as injections and added to the feed. Again, there is an economic basis for this indiscriminate use of medication and that is to prevent the animals from getting sick.

"It is becoming apparent now, however, that this practice has contributed to the development of antibiotic-resistant super bugs. In fact, there is a movement underway that will eliminate the same type of antibiotics used to treat disease in humans from being used on animals. The difference at my ranch is that I treat only animals that need treatment and we don't give sub-therapeutic levels of antibiotics to healthy animals."

"What?" Tracy began, but Michael got up from the table and came around to her side and kissed her soundly on the mouth.

"Enough for one lesson. You have to come out my way to learn more."

"Let's call it a night, then," Tracy suggested, grinning mischievously.

"Good idea, I'm beat. It's been a very long day for me," Michael answered, stifling a yawn. "And all this talking has plumb wore me out."

"I'll just take a quick shower." There was a trace of laughter in her voice as she tiptoed and returned his kiss.

Tracy turned on the shower, letting the water get warm while she removed her make-up. This would be one of the quickest showers she had taken in recent memory. She slid open the shower door and stuck one foot in, testing the water temperature, then decided to turn on more cold water. Stepping in, she hurriedly shampooed her hair and lathered herself from face to toe, using her best shower gel.

Wrapped in a large plush bath towel, Tracy hurriedly blow-dried her hair, then sprayed a hint of her favorite fragrance in vital spots. Steam left a cloud on the mirror, so she wiped one area until the mirror squeaked, clearing a space to see her image. One last scrunch of her hair and she opened the bathroom door. She was just about to speak to Michael when she noticed he was curled up on one side of the bed in his underwear, sound asleep. He looked so peaceful.

Tracy stood looking down at Michael. She considered waking him but decided against it. Was it disappointment or his fatigue that stopped her? All of a sudden Tracy realized it was neither; rather, she felt a sense of relief he was asleep. *What does that mean? Is our relationship so unremarkable that the passion has gone? Or is it something else?*

Hoping it was nothing more than fatigue with them both, Tracy slid in beside him and kissed him on the cheek. " 'Night, dear Michael," she whispered.

"Well, you were a barrel of laughs last night," Tracy teased as she bent over and gave his hair a tousle. "Rise and shine, sleepy-head, the world awaits."

"Awaits what?" Michael mumbled.

"I don't know, I've just heard that said so many times I thought it was a good line."

Michael turned on his side and rose on one elbow. He ran long bronze fingers through his tangled hair and clenched his teeth together, stifling a yawn.

"Sorry about that, Trace. It was a long, rough day yesterday. After the red-eye flight, I had meetings until about two o'clock." He grinned at her sheepishly as he patted the bed beside him. "Come on back in here and I'll make it up to you."

Tracy slowly tugged her nightshirt over her head and was about to climb back into bed when the phone rang. She hesitated.

"Don't answer it."

Sitting on the edge of the bed, she looked at the phone then turned back to Michael and shrugged, "I'll just see who it is and be brief."

"You want the good news first, or the bad?" Nick asked on the other end of the line.

Chapter Seven

"There's both?" Tracy's voice rose in surprise. Putting her hand over the mouthpiece, she whispered to Michael, "It's the P.I. friend of mine. I think it's important." Then to Nick, "Gimme the bad first."

"Your little old friend has busted out of the hospital. No one knows where he went or how long he's been gone. When they checked on him this morning he'd split. I'm still tracking his background. It's a bit murky at this point." Tracy heard the sound of papers being shuffled, then he continued, " I found a trail of sorts on him and it goes back to Berlin. It may tell us how he is tied in with your Samuel. I think I'll start there. I've booked a trip on Wednesday of next week. I have a little more to do here first." Nick paused, then he said, "Now for the good news, I checked out the info you had on the Steinfelds through utility records and the post office. It is correct. It's just three blocks from the original address. Good going, Trace."

"That's marvelous! I can find out where Hannah is from the Steinfelds." Tracy exclaimed. "Thanks for your help. Keep me posted on anything else you might find, especially on the other man. Somehow I think they are all linked but I can't figure out how."

"I have a contact in Denver and I could get him to go over to their house in Rapid City."

"Don't do that. They might get scared and disappear on me like the family did when Mr. Levine was looking for them. I don't want to take a chance."

"Have a little faith in your old pal, huh? My contact is a smooth operator and will find out whatever you need to know about her."

"No, I would rather do that myself and right away. I have something to give Hannah and I'm curious to see if she remembers anything about her father. And I'd like to find out her story."

Michael climbed out of bed and made his way to the bathroom, grabbing his duffel bag on the way. He needed a good shave. This was a good time to do that. Tracy would be busy for a while and he had to catch a plane in— he looked at his watch— three and a half hours. The shuttle would take two hours with the stops and he liked to be at the airport at least an hour and a half before he had to board. Today he would be lucky to get there with an hour to spare.

Tracy was just hanging up the phone when Michael emerged from the bathroom.

"I take it the daughter has been found?"

"Well, almost. They found a Sidney Steinfeld at the address I gave them. He will know where Hannah is— Hey, I thought we had something to take care of."

"Sorry, love, I've got a plane to catch in three hours and I have to reserve a space on the shuttle. Can you take me to catch it?"

"You won't make it in time if you take the shuttle. Let me get dressed and I'll take you to the airport. That way I'll get to spend a little more time with you. Besides, I can book my flight to South Dakota while I'm there."

"You'll get a better deal on-line."

"I don't like to use my credit card on-line unless I absolutely have to. I'm always hearing about those hackers and I just don't trust all that business."

"You have to move into the twenty-first century, my dear, and that includes the electronic age." Michael laughed and swatted her on the rear.

"In my own good time. I have made some concessions and I'll get there eventually."

* * * * * * * * *

Jack ran the back of his hand across his mouth and checked it for blood. He started to protest, but decided against it. Instead, he cowered on the sand where he had fallen after the old man hit him.

"You can't do anything right, you idiot. After that stunt with the car, I thought we had everything settled." Rutger Dietrick spoke through clenched teeth, his voice low and angry. He circled Jack, stopping to lean down inches from Jack's face. His eyes glittered with outrage. "I told you if you failed me again— "

Marcos shuddered and sank further back in the corner. He was relieved, having escaped the dressing down Jack was receiving, but he knew he was probably next. His eyes sought an avenue of escape, but one evil glance from Dietrick discouraged him.

"I no longer need your services; I've made other arrangements." Dietrick reached into his pocket and pulled out a gun.

Jack jumped to his feet. "Wait. One more chance. I promise we'll—" He cowered, backing against the wall of the cave. Terror drained his strength; he fell to his knees, whimpering.

Dietrick looked at Marcos. "I have one more chore for you."

Marcos cried in relief. He had more time to figure out a way to escape because he knew, once the "chore" had been completed, he would be next. As the shot rang out, Marcos flinched in horror. He checked his body for a wound, then looked up to see Jack crumpled on the ground, a pool of blood staining wider circles on the sand.

* * * * * * * * *

A day later Tracy walked outside the terminal in Rapid City, South Dakota, near the Badlands and Mount Rushmore and, she hoped, Hannah. The late afternoon sun made her squint as she looked for the rental car she had arranged earlier. The car was a late model four-door white sedan, about as nondescript as one could get. She pushed the button on the key ring, unlocking the doors, then placed her luggage on the rear seat and climbed in behind the wheel. She sat a moment and studied the maps the clerk had printed out for her. One was to the motel near the airport; the other was to Sidney's house.

First she would check into her room, call Sidney and make an appointment to see him in the morning, and then have dinner. It would be an early night for her and hopefully, tomorrow she could wrap up this case and fly over to North Dakota for a short visit with Michael.

Tracy unpacked the few clothes she brought. When they were put away she placed the call to Sidney. The voice on the answering machine sounded a little younger than what she calculated Sidney to be, but perhaps it was his son. She left her name, phone number, extension and stated she was from Monet Cove, California and had some important information for him. Would Sidney please call her as soon as possible? Tracy decided against dinner and looked forward to crawling into bed and getting a good night's sleep.

Half the next day had passed since Tracy called and left the message on the answering machine. She was beginning to get worried and thought about just driving over to the residence. Maybe she would give him a bit longer, at least until she had eaten. If she heard nothing by then she was going to Sidney's house. Sitting around the motel room waiting for something that might not happen didn't appeal to her.

Tracy grabbed her purse from the dresser and hurried out the door. She checked to make sure it locked behind her and headed toward the coffee shop. Afraid Sidney would call, she had skipped breakfast and now her stomach began to rumble and fuss.

The waitress waved her to a table and brought over the menu. Tracy ordered a grilled chicken salad with ranch dressing and a glass of iced tea. When her food arrived she ate quickly but without relish. Instead her mind churned, going over all that happened in the last week or so. So many questions left unanswered, so many puzzles to piece together. She was suddenly afraid not all the answers would be found.

Tracy counted out the money and left it on the table. She scooted the chair back and rummaged through her purse looking for her sunglasses. Not finding them, she headed back to her room, thinking she had left them there.

The phone was ringing when she walked through the door.

"This is Tracy Chapman."

"I hear you have some information for me. What is this all about?" The man on the other end of the phone asked.

"I would rather deliver it in person if that's all right with you."

Tracy could hear a muffled conversation as he covered the phone and conferred with someone else.

"Maybe you could tell me something about your information and yourself. You have to admit this sounds a bit suspicious."

"It possibly pertains to a relative of yours who recently passed away. I work with the medical examiner's office in California and we are trying to locate next of kin."

" I don't believe we have family members in California." His voice was courteous but held a tone of caution.

"It won't take a minute of your time to just verify the facts for me. I've come a long way to turn back now."

There was a long silence followed by more muffled conversation with the other person. "I prefer to come and meet you at your motel. They have a coffee shop there."

"That will be fine. How soon could I expect you?"

"In about an hour. I— we just got home and brought lunch with us."

"I'll meet you in the coffee shop in an hour, then."

Tracy could hardly control her enthusiasm. Finally she would be able to find Hannah and reunite another family. It would be good to have the hoodlums off her back as well. Surely, once this was all settled, the family would be able to shed some light on the rest of the mystery.

She turned on the television for background noise and glanced at the clock every ten minutes. Finally, forty minutes later, she tucked the journal and letters into her briefcase and headed to the coffee shop in case Sidney was early.

"Miss Chapman?"

"Yes," Tracy answered and turned in her chair. Immediately her heart sank. The man was too young. The Sidney she was looking for would be in his eighties, at least.

"I'm Sid Steinfeld and this is my wife, Julie."

Confused, Tracy stared at the two then stammered, "Please. Have a seat. I'm afraid I'm really— I— you're younger than— Sid Steinfeld, Sidney Steinfeld?"

"Yes," Sid said, a half smile crossed his face, "You must have gotten me confused with my uncle. His name was Sidney Steinfeld, too."

"And Hannah? I'm looking for a woman involved with his family. Her name was Hannah Levine and I believe Sidney and his wife adopted her."

"Sidney Steinfeld is a common name in this part of the country. I'm afraid I can't help you find this Hannah." Sid suddenly stood up and moved behind his wife's chair. "Well, no problem. I hope you find who you are looking for."

"Wait. Does your uncle live around here?"

"I'm afraid he passed away years ago. Sorry." He took his wife's arm and led her toward the door.

They were gone before Tracy could recover from her disappointment. She signaled the waitress she was leaving and hurried to the door just as the couple's sedan pulled from the parking lot onto the street.

Strange, she thought, *why did they rush off like that?* But then there was no reason for them to stay either, since they weren't the people she was looking for. *I suppose I would do the same if the situation were reversed*, she mused.

Tracy walked back to her room. Maybe she could call later and see if he could give her any information about his uncle's family. She dug into her purse for her card key, and then dropped it. She snatched up the card and jammed it into the slot. It didn't work, so she carefully, slowly pushed it into the slot and pulled it out again. When the light changed to green, she quickly opened the door. Throwing her purse and briefcase on the chair, she sank down on the bed, wanting to cry.

The phone rang and she grabbed it, thinking maybe the Steinfelds had changed their mind about helping her.

"Trace, I have some bad news for you," Nick yelled into the phone above the noise surrounding him. "I'm at your place and someone broke in. I heard the call on the police band and recognized your address."

"How bad is it?"

"The place is a mess both downstairs in the store and in your private quarters. I don't know if they found what they were looking for. Amy is here and she has taken an inventory of sorts. It doesn't appear any of the items in your shop are missing. Any idea what they were looking for?"

"Oh, my God! Is there much damage?" Tracy gasped, realizing a shiver of panic.

"Not really, just things strewn everywhere. Drawers were emptied and the contents scattered about. What were they looking for, Tracy?" He repeated.

"I'm not sure. How did they get in?"

"Through the back door, beach side. They probably left that way, too, because when the police came on scene after the alarm went off, the perpetrators got out just ahead of them. It took a little longer for the police to get here because they were at the scene of a major accident. So, whoever broke in here had a little time to go through a lot of your stuff and it wasn't a lone burglar. There had to be more than one person to do all this in the amount of time they had."

"Let me speak with Amy; then I want to talk to you again."

Tracy heard Nick calling Amy to the phone, but a male voice came on the other end of the line.

"Miss Chapman, this is Officer Helmsley. I understand you've been informed of the break-in. According to Miss Bryant, there doesn't seem to be anything missing and the damage is minimal. Any idea who might have done this, or what they were looking for? They must have been looking for a specific item because even with all the expensive antiques around, they didn't bother to take anything. Of course, we don't know about your private dwelling and there's no way of telling until you check things out. When will you be returning?"

"I'll try to get a flight out as soon as possible. Do you think they will be back and did they break the lock on the door? Can you lock the place up until I get back home?"

"It's hard to say if they'll return. The lock will need to be fixed, but your friend Nicholas said he would stay and make sure things are safe until you get back." For a minute the officer was distracted, then he said that Amy was ready to talk to her.

"They sure made a mess, Tracy. I'm going to close the shop and get things straightened out."

"What time did it happen?"

"They came in around five o'clock this morning. That's when the alarm went off. That's why I wasn't here and they were able to have some time to do all this. The police have been on scene since five-thirty, but they just got in touch with me about a couple of hours ago. They had to wait for the crime scene investigators to get here and do their work. It's nine-thirty here now."

"Thank God you weren't there. How did the police get in touch with you?"

"Nick phoned me after he heard the call on the police scanner. He knew they would want someone to check and see if anything was missing after they did the initial investigation. They didn't want anything disturbed before then."

"Let me talk to Nick again. Oh, Amy, thanks for your help. I'll see you soon."

"Hey, sunshine." Nick came back on the line.

"Do you think they'll be back?"

"We have things pretty well under control here. I'll hang around and keep a watch until you get back."

"Thanks, Nick. Sounds like you're kinda busy at the moment. I shouldn't be here too much longer."

"Trace, be careful. I don't like the smell of this. I think you bit off more than was safe this time."

"Oh, you always say that," she chided, although the cheery banter didn't quite measure up. She decided against telling him of her failure here. She would discuss that with him when she got home.

Tracy replaced the receiver, her hand remaining on the instrument letting the news sink in. She wondered how much worse this day could get. Picking up the phone again, she dialed for an outside line and put in the numbers for the airport. There were no seats left on the two flights leaving the rest of the day, so she made reservations for tomorrow. She depressed the button and dialed Sid's number.

The phone rang four times and Tracy was about to hang up rather than leave a message. "Hello," Sid answered breathlessly.

"Did your uncle adopt a girl named Hannah?"

"Look, Miss Chapman, I don't know who you are or what you hope to gain, but you yourself said we weren't the people you were looking for. Just leave us alone." With that he hung up.

"I should have known it wouldn't be this simple. Serves me right for not checking further," Tracy quickly chastised herself. She was usually more thorough in her research, but then everything had seemed to correspond.

Refusing to accept defeat, Tracy grabbed her purse and headed for the motel office. "Could you tell me where the graveyard is?"

The young woman looked at Tracy as if she had two heads. "Graveyard?"

"Yes, where they bury people." The words came out more harshly than Tracy had intended. The break-in was the last straw today and left her in a bad mood.

"It's about three miles north of here. You follow that road out there for a quarter mile then turn left on the farm road. If you stay on that road you can't miss it."

"Thanks," Tracy called over her shoulder and hurried out the door. She wasn't sure of finding what she was looking for, but she was definitely going to cover as much ground as possible before tomorrow's flight. It was obvious the nephew wasn't going to help her. One would think, after all these years, the fear of being found would've vanished. After all, it wasn't as if Hannah was still a child to be taken away from the family. She just couldn't figure out his attitude. Steinfeld obviously knew more than he was telling. He was too abrupt, too unwilling to talk to her. He hadn't even been curious enough to find out why she thought he could help her.

Tracy spent the better part of an hour looking at tombstones, to no avail. Back in her car she was driving toward the exit when she spotted a building in the corner of the cemetery. It was almost hidden by a wall of hedges and large shade trees. If there was an office, surely they had a record of all who were interred here.

"Sidney Steinfeld?" the man asked, his finger moving down the list a second time. "No, I don't have a Sidney Steinfeld here."

"Thanks." Nothing but dead ends, she thought. "Excuse me, but is it possible he could be anywhere else?"

"Not unless he passed in a different city."

"Thanks for your time." Tracy started out the door, then turned and asked, "Do you have a genealogy society here?"

"There is the South Dakota Genealogy Society. I'll look up the address and telephone number for you. "

"You're a doll!" she called over her shoulder as she hurried from the office with the information in hand. "Sometimes you just have to rely on the old-fashioned method," Tracy said aloud, driving out the cemetery gates.

After two hours searching through books, Tracy was just about to give up when she found the family history she was looking for. Sidney Steinfeld had died in Hastings, Nebraska, on November 13,1960. Also, she found that their daughter, Hannah had married one Irwin Strasberg June 1950, in Hastings, also.

Tracy closed the book and rubbed her eyes. She returned the books and asked, "Is there a library close by?"

"Yes, two blocks down on the left side of the street. Did you find what you were looking for?"

"I did, thank you."

Now, to sign on to a computer provided by the local library and access the Website she frequented that would give her an address in

Hastings. As Tracy turned into the library's parking lot her phone rang.

"Trace, I hate to do this to you but you need to come home as soon as you can." The urgency in Nick Gregor's voice raised the fine hair on Tracy's neck as an oddly primitive warning sounded in her brain.

"What's wrong?"

"They found the body of Jack Holgate floating in the cove. He's one of the hoodlums that broke into your place."

Chapter Eight

"Did he drown? Was it an accident?" Even as Tracy asked, she knew what the answer would be and a wave of apprehension swept over her.

"At this point it was either that or the bullet hole through his back and I'm betting on the latter." Nick paused. "In all seriousness, we have to wait for the medical examiner's conclusion to find out what really killed him, but either way, he was murdered. According to the police, he wasn't supposed to be found, but the plan didn't work out so well. Hang on a minute." There was silence for what seemed a long time and then Nick was back on the phone. "When you make your flight arrangements call and give me the information. I want to pick you up in San Jose when you come in."

" I'm booked on a flight tomorrow, but I can go out to the airport and see if I can get on standby for today."

"Then call me when you are boarding and I'll see you on this end." There was silence again then he added, "Trace, watch your back."

"I will. See you soon." Slamming the car in reverse, she backed out of the parking spot.

Tracy tossed her keys on the bed and dialed the airport. As she listened to the menu she pressed the proper number on the telephone keypad and another when prompted. This was one of the most aggravating things about the new electronic age, trying to get any information by a phone call. After pushing several more numbers and listening to all kinds of announcements, she finally learned there was a plane leaving for San Jose at four-twenty this afternoon. It would arrive in San Jose at 11:30 tonight with a change in Denver, Colorado.

Tracy checked her watch. It was now three o'clock. She would have enough time to pack and get to the airport to secure her place on the standby list. Hopefully, even though it was Saturday and only one other flight, the plane might have an empty seat. Maybe someone would cancel.

"Tracy Chapman, please return to the podium at gate three. Tracy Chapman, please return to the podium at gate three."

The announcement startled Tracy and she quickly made her way to the podium. Boarding had already begun and she hoped this would be good news.

"We have a seat for you. If you'll just give me your ticket we'll get you on board as quickly as possible."

"Thanks, I really appreciate this." Finally, something was going right.

It seemed she had just nodded off when the pilot slowed down the engines and lowered the landing gear. Tracy looked out the window. The lights of San Jose glittered like a carpet of diamonds below. A string of automobile lights indicated a back up on the freeway and she wondered if Nick was caught in the traffic jam. Further ahead, she spotted the flashing lights of emergency vehicles and ahead of them the freeway was clear for a short distance. An accident had caused the back up.

A long ragged sigh escaped her lips as they touched down on the runway. She was always relieved to be at the end of her journey and safely on the ground once again. The man in the next seat turned and looked at her. When he noted she was okay, he pulled out his cell phone and waited for the announcement authorizing its use.

As she walked into the terminal, Tracy scanned the faces in the crowd. Not one to be confined, Nick would probably be standing near the back. She scooted around a young mother who bent down and scooped up her toddler out of harm's way. Another collision was avoided when she went around an elderly woman who had stopped in mid-stream of the human traffic to greet her grandchild. It was then she saw Nick leaning against a pillar, smiling as he watched her maneuver through the sea of bodies.

"Here, let me take that," Nick said, taking her bag. "Do you have any more?"

"No, I travel light." Tracy gave him a hug. "Thanks for meeting me, but I could've taken the shuttle."

"I don't think that would be a good idea right now, especially since it would have been pretty late when you got home."

"Any new developments?"

"It's too soon for the autopsy results and I imagine whoever shot Holgate wouldn't want another incident right now.""

"You think it might be gang related?"

"Those two thugs have a long criminal history for their age. I'm not absolutely sure they were gang members, or if this was a gang hit, though. One may have done the other one in; there's no real honor among crooks these days. Until we find out, I'm going to be your shadow."

"That won't be necessary, Nick. I can handle myself."

"I'm sure you can, but four eyes are better'n two." They were in the parking lot and Nick touched Tracy's elbow, steering her down the aisle where he was parked.

Traveling to Monet Cove, Tracy told Nick about her trip. "I hope you'll be more successful on your trip than I was, especially now." Tracy shifted in her seat and watched Nick's face as she continued, "I think this is more than just an interest in an antique desk, or whatever else they might think Samuel Levine had of value. How about you?"

"Yep, but I don't have the foggiest idea at the moment what that might be. Which brings up another point. While I'm gone I've arranged for a buddy of mine to keep you safe. He's an ex-cop and I trust him with my life." He turned and winked at her. "And yours."

"Nick— "

"No use arguing. I gotta know you're safe or I can't leave. Which will it be; me stay here until they settle this, or go to Germany and hopefully find out the root of the evil?"

"You're right. You're always right, of course."

"I've set up a cot at the back of your shop and I'll sleep there for a couple of days. I think if you stay close to home while I get ready for this trip, you should be okay. Amy will be there with you."

"But I— "

"Promise me."

"All right, I promise."

"Somehow I don't quite believe you."

"I'll be fine, you'll see. Anyway, I need to do an inventory there at the shop and maybe Amy and I can interview some people for the new place."

The next couple of days were busy ones for both Nick and Tracy, but at the end of each day Nick returned to the shop. Amy and Tracy hired a woman, fully qualified to run the new shop, much to their delight. They had also settled on a name: Tymes Two.

Nick, in the meantime, completed preparations for his trip. He made a copy of the Levine family photograph and wrote down their home address in Germany listed on the expired passport. He also brought his friend by to familiarize himself with Tracy's place.

Shane Mulligan was in his early fifties, tall and lean. His hair was now almost completely grey, with only a hint of its original copper color and his blue-grey eyes seemed ever alert beneath the thick silver eyebrows. He strolled forward and extended a hand when introduced to Tracy and Amy.

"Pleasure, ladies," he greeted. "Quite a place you have here. Nice stuff."

"We think our selection of antiques is quite adequate," Tracy answered, a hint of censure in her voice. Amy, on the other hand, seemed to find him quite fascinating and suppressed a giggle at his choice of words.

"Right," Shane answered and grimaced in good humor.

Nick raised an eyebrow at Tracy's behavior, and then addressed Shane. "There's a small cot in the back room. It's comfortable in spite of its size. You shouldn't have to sleep here too long and I'm sure the ladies will do everything they can to make your stay an easy one. Right, Tracy?"

"Everything." Tracy felt like a child being introduced to her babysitter and resentment reared its ugly head. She appreciated Nick's concern and Shane's willingness to help, but she understood the danger involved in her life right now and was prepared to be ever vigilant. "By the way, Nick, how about the other fellow who hung out with what's-his-name— er, Jack?" she asked, changing the subject.

"Marcos? The police checked at the address they had on record and he has simply disappeared. His sister said he was in a state of panic when he grabbed some of his things and took off. He told her he would be out of town for a while. She said she had never seen him so frightened."

"Maybe he's the one who shot Jack. They could've had a falling out."

"Dunno. Time will tell, hopefully. In the meantime, I would appreciate your full cooperation with Shane." Watching Shane and Amy disappear into the rear of the shop, he added, "You be nice to my friend while I'm gone and don't go gettin' pig-headed on me."

"Whatever do you mean?" Tracy batted her eyelashes and gave him an impish grin.

"I mean it, Tracy. And what the hell was that put-down a minute ago?"

"I'm sorry. Of course you are right and I'll apologize to Shane when he comes back. I certainly don't want to start out on the wrong foot with him, especially since Amy seems quite taken with him."

"I didn't notice."

"No, you were too busy watching my reactions, but I love you just the same." She reached up and tousled his hair affectionately, dismissing the whole issue.

True to her word, Tracy apologized to Shane when he and Amy reappeared. Shane seemed as though he wasn't sure why, but he gave her a nod, accepting the apology. "Did Amy fill you in on the alarm as she gave you the grand tour?" Shane nodded again and Tracy tossed a smile at Nick, letting him know she was behaving herself.

"Nick, can I see you off tomorrow?"

"Nope, I'm taking a red-eye out to save you some money on the ticket. I'll call once I'm there and again as soon as I find out anything. In the meantime, mind your manners and watch your back."

"You be careful and don't step on any toes over there. I don't want to have to come over and bail you out of the pokey." Although she smiled broadly, there was a hint of concern in her tone.

Two days passed after Nick left for Germany before he finally called. He gave Tracy the name and phone number of the hotel where he was staying and told her he would call her in a few days, hopefully with some information. The connection was bad so he didn't talk long, but did make her promise to call him if there were any new developments in the case. When the results of the autopsy came through it was no surprise the exact cause of Jack's death was from the bullet wound in his back. The bullet had severed his spine and destroyed most of his internal organs. Death had been almost instantaneous.

There had been no water in his lungs even though his body had been in the ocean. Upon searching up and down the beach and from parking lot to the ocean, they found no evidence at the location where his body was discovered. The police determined he was killed elsewhere. Tracy called Nick but he was out, so she left a message on the phone in his room. There was no need to talk to him at this point anyway, just relay the information.

Another day passed before Tracy heard from Nick again and she was starting to get nervous. "I can't say I'm surprised at the findings on the murder. I'll check in with the police department when I get back. Maybe they'll know something by then." Nick moved the phone to his other hand and continued, "I've covered a lot of ground and attracted some attention, but I didn't find out a lot. Those people still around don't remember too much about that time, or are reluctant to talk about it.

"The neighborhood where he lived is all fairly new now, but there is a fellow still living that may know something. I'm meeting him on my way to the airport. Anyway, I'll fill you in when I get back, which should be in about thirty-six hours. I'm checking out of the hotel now and will be incommunicado until I touch down in the States."

There were clicks and a lot of static before Nick's voice could be heard again. He gave her his flight information and ended the conversation with, "I can't say too much more as the walls have ears and I'm not sure who they belong to. I can say though, when you do something, you do it up pretty good. Stay low and I'll see you soon."

"Be— " Tracy began, but the phone went dead. "Careful," she finished, and suddenly felt uneasy about having sent Nick to Germany. She wasn't sure why. Nick was a big boy and could take care of himself quite well, but this was getting ugly and Germany was a long way from home.

Nick hung up the phone and finished packing his bags. He was relieved to be finally going home. He was getting too old to keep ahead of the tails especially those he acquired since coming to Germany. He wasn't sure who they were or what they wanted, but they were obvious and very persistent.

He patted his breast coat pocket making sure his passport and airline tickets were there when a slight noise in the hallway made him hesitate. Hearing nothing more, he turned back to the bed and zipped up the large bag. Nick tossed the strap over his shoulder and checked the room for items he might have missed. A knock sounded at the door. He placed the bag back on the bed and quietly crossed the room.

"Mr. Greger, I've come for your bags."

Nick looked through the peek-hole and saw a bellman with a luggage rack. He pulled some bills from his pocket and opened the door. "I can handle them, thanks." As he extended his hand with the tip, two very large men blocked the doorway, one of which pointed a gun at him. The other man slipped the bellman some money and the bellman stuck the bills in his pocket and strutted down the hallway, his mouth slipping into an easy grin.

"You will come with us, Mr. Greger."

Nick tried to close the door but the man with the gun pushed it open again, taking Nick by the arm. "I'm coming. Don't get so huffy." He turned back to grab his bag, but the man jerked him around.

"Leave it. That will be taken care of."

"I've been out of practice too long," Nick stated, shaking his head. "A few years ago you wouldn't have taken me so easy."

Tracy paced the terminal, waiting for Nick's plane to land. According to the lady at the ticket counter, it had been delayed in New York. She was glad he was back in the United States and anxious to hear what he'd found out. She hoped he would call from New York and give her an update on his flight, but perhaps he had been sitting on a grounded plane, or awaiting more information. At any rate his plane should be touching down any minute.

"Trans National Airways, flight 1632 is now landing," came the announcement, as if right on cue. Tracy moved to the edge of the ramp down which the passengers would be coming. She jockeyed for an unhampered view among the crowd waiting for the same flight. The passengers emerged sporadically in groups and Tracy moved continuously to allow families and friends to greet each other.

As the number of passengers slowed, Tracy again felt uneasy. Had Nick missed the plane? Surely he would have called and let her know. She began to pace again and took out her cell phone. She called her house and punched in the code to retrieve any messages. There was none. Seeing a lone man coming down the ramp, Tracy approached him, "Were you on flight 1632?" The man nodded and kept walking. "Are there any more passengers?"

"No, I'm it." He looked briefly over his shoulder at her and continued walking.

"Thanks." Strange and disquieting thoughts began to race through her mind. What if he had an accident in Germany and was lying in a hospital bed, or worse? Maybe the ears he mentioned were unfriendly ones and he disappeared because of something he might have revealed in a telephone conversation. No, Nick was like a cat, he always landed on his feet, something like that could never happen to him. She would just have to go home and wait for him to call, but first she checked with the staff at the ticket counter to find out if another plane was expected tonight.

"No, that's the last flight until tomorrow morning at ten-forty."

"Thanks." Tracy swept an errant strand of hair behind her ear and headed out of the terminal. Shane Mulligan pushed off from the pillar against which he had been leaning and fell into step beside her.

"Where's Nick?"

"He wasn't on that flight and there isn't another one tonight. I think I'll call the hotel in Germany when we get home and see if he checked out yet. I wouldn't put it past him to have missed the flight." But there was no conviction in her voice.

The ride home was a silent one until Shane finally tried to put her at ease. "I wouldn't worry about old Nick if I were you. He's been around the block more'n once and he can handle himself. He may have gotten a lead at the last minute."

"Perhaps you're right. After all, what trouble could he have gotten into in this day and age?"

Tracy dialed the number to Nick's hotel. The desk clerk answered in German. "Do you speak English?"

"Yes, Miss."

"Could you please connect me with Nicholas Greger's room?"

"One moment, please." There was the sound of pages being turned and the clerk came back on the line. "I'm sorry, Miss, but what was the name again?"

Tracy started to repeat the name she had given then said, "Maybe it's under Nicholas Greger— G.r.e.g.e.r."

"I'm sorry, Miss, but there is no such person here."

"Then he checked out already. Could you tell me when he checked out?"

"That person was never registered here, Miss." A pause on the line, then, "Is there something else I can help you with?"

"Are you sure about that? I talked to him several times and he was calling from your hotel. I called there once myself and the call was transferred to his room."

"I'm sorry, Miss," the desk clerk repeated, "perhaps he was staying with someone here. In that event I would have no way of checking for you if he was never reported to us."

Tracy was silent for a moment, "If for some reason he should show up, could you tell him to get in touch with Tracy Chapman? I sure would appreciate it."

"Yes, Miss Chapman. Thank you for calling Hotel Gisbad."

Chapter Nine

The car in which Nick was abducted careened around a curve. Tires squealed in protest as it made a sharp right turn. It raced through narrow streets and back alleyways, drawing little attention from the pedestrians. Surprisingly, Nick's eyes had not been covered. Whoever these people were, they were not trying to keep their route a secret. Of course, he would never be able to find the way again, or tell anyone where he was taken. Hell, he didn't even have time to read the street signs.

Almost certainly these men were not with the police; even in a foreign country they would follow a certain procedure. Besides, Nick had committed no crime, at least none that he was aware of.

"Who are you guys?" Nick asked.

"All in good time," the man next to him answered. He sat forward and braced himself with a hand clutched to the front seat. All the while his gaze continually shifted from the windshield to the back window.

The car slowed to a more manageable speed and pulled up in front of a warehouse. The driver sounded the horn and a metal door was slowly cranked upward, allowing them to enter.

As Nick's eyes became accustomed to the darkness he noticed a crane moving slowly high above the floor where a few grimy windows filtered the light coming in. Huge cartons were stacked from floor to ceiling further blocking the light. The three men led him around and through the maze of cartons toward the back, then up some stairs into a dingy office. A flimsy wooden chair was pulled out and Nick was directed to sit.

The office was tiny, without windows and only the one door. A heavy set man sat behind a desk, seemingly too occupied to take note of their entry. A second man stood outside the door, while a third stood behind the chair in which Nick had been placed. Escape was out of the question, at least for the time being. Perhaps if they moved him somewhere else later—

"Here he is, Otto. He was just leaving for the airport when we got there."

Otto was bent over a stack of paperwork and all Nick could see of him was his black hair, which stood on end as though ruffled by fingers raked through it. When Otto finally looked up from the light-shrouded desk he squinted, waiting for his eyes to adjust to the poor light in the rest of the room.

His brown eyes held a gleam of interest as he focused on Nick. "Good work," and to Nick, " We'll get right down to it. How are you connected with Herr Mueller?"

"Who?"

"Herr Karl Mueller. What business do you have with him?"

"Sorry, buddy, but I think there has been a mistake made here. I'm looking for information about a Rutger Dietrick. I don't know a Karl Mueller," he lied.

The two Germans exchanged glances before Otto spoke again. "We believe they are the same. Again I ask you, what is your business with him?"

Nick was silent a minute then decided to tell the truth, to a point. "Rutger Dietrick has become a little over zealous about my friend's client and I came over here to find out about his background. I'm not aware of any laws I've broken in the process."

"Mr— " Otto checked some papers in front of him and his square jaw tensed visibly, "—Greger, your life is in danger because of questions you have been asking, or rather those you have approached with your questions. This Mueller is a very bad person. He has some equally bad friends still around here." He took off his glasses and pinched the bridge of his nose. "Please share with us the knowledge you have of this person. Where is he right now, who is your friend's client and why is Mueller interested in this person?"

"If I knew why he was interested, I wouldn't be over here asking questions about him." Nick shifted in his chair and leaned toward the desk, "Dietrick— Mueller— he's just a little old man. How dangerous can he be?"

"Don't let his age and stature fool you. The mere mention of his name brings terror to the hearts of those still around who remember the things he has done. I can assure you he has not lost the ability to bring more terror."

"Otto." A young woman stuck her head in the doorway, interrupting the conversation. She crossed over to the desk and bent down to whisper in Otto's ear then she left the room as suddenly as she had entered.

Otto stood up and started from the room. "You know what to do," he said matter-of-factly to the man standing behind Nick.

Chapter Ten

A heavy curtain of fog drifted in from the sea, casting a dreary pall over the usually sunny morning. The gloom mirrored Tracy's mood. Nightmares had robbed her of a good night's sleep and worries about Nick filled her waking hours. Two days had passed since he was supposed to come home— if only she could hear from him. She leaned against the railing of her deck and looked out into the fog as though answers might be lurking there.

A big sigh escaped her lips and she started to go inside. The dark silhouette of a person standing in the fog caught her attention and she turned back. Tracy couldn't tell if the person was facing her or not and she stared harder. As suddenly as it had appeared the figure disappeared, swallowed up by the swirling haze.

Tracy stood a minute more to see if the figure returned before she went inside. She hadn't looked up Hannah's address yet. At least that would take up some time. Firing up her computer, she entered Hannah's name. Since she had the right name this time it took only moments for the information to come up; her address, area code, phone number, birth date and the name of several possible relatives, the first of which was a Sarah Adams. She printed out the page and placed it in her purse.

Tracy considered giving Hannah a call, but in the end decided against it for several reasons. First, she never liked giving bad news over the phone. Even though the daughter hadn't been in touch with her father for such a long time, and memories of him so distant she probably no longer knew him, he was still her father. Second, perhaps the family would disappear again. She certainly had gotten the run around from the nephew.

A crash and loud voices from downstairs brought Tracy to her feet. She ran downstairs in time to find Shane chasing a figure through the back door. And, as before, the fog swallowed up the figure.

"Who was that?"

Shane stopped and rubbed the back of his head. "I don't know, but he packs a good wallop. I don't think he expected to find me here. He picked up something and slammed me back here. When I didn't go down he decided not to pursue whatever he came here for." Shane sat down, still rubbing the back of his head. "I sure saw stars for a minute, though."

Tracy examined his injury. A lump was already forming. "Here, watch my finger?" She held up her index finger and moved it slowly in front of him, from one side to the other.

"What's that supposed to tell you?" Shane laughed.

"I think it has something to do with the way your eyes move. I'm not sure, but I've seen it done many times when someone gets hit on the head. You seem to be able to follow my finger all right. I think you need to get to the doctor and have him take a look just in case."

"I've had a lot worse. I'll be fine." Shane ran his hand over his head, then traced the bump with the tips of his fingers. "Is there any blood? It sure feels like it." He pulled his hand back and checked it to see for himself.

"Did you get a good look at him?"

"No, just a flash before he turned and beat it out of here. I think he was elderly, but he sure moved fast for a senior citizen," Shane said grudgingly. "There was no point in trying to find him in that soup out there. Do you think it was that Dietrick fellow?"

"As far as I know he and the surviving hoodlum are the only ones interested in my house."

"I'll call the police."

"What's the point? They won't be able to find him either and by the time they get here he'll probably be long gone." Tracy let out a long audible breath. "I wish I knew what he was after. I have gone over the desk and all of Samuel's personal effects thoroughly. I found nothing that would draw this much interest."

A car door slammed out front. Shane checked his watch, "Oh good, there's Amy. She's a little late and I was worried about her driving to work in the fog." He walked to the front door and opened it, waiting for her to come in. "Hey!" he called and hurried out the door.

Tracy followed him out. "What's wrong?"

"A car just pulled away and I think it might have been our intruder. I can't imagine why he stayed around." Shane ran along the sidewalk to Amy's car. The door stood open, but she was not inside. He looked up and down the street, at least as far as he could see clearly. There was no sign of her. "Dammit! He's taken Amy. She must've pulled up as he was leaving."

"But what would he want from her?" Tracy asked, coming up behind him. "Do you think he'll hurt her? Let's call the police. Did you get a look at the license plate?" Questions tumbled forth as Tracy was suddenly filled with fear. "What are you doing?"

"I'm going to see if I can find them," Shane called over his shoulder.

"But you can't see anything in this fog. Wait, I'll come with you."

"Stay here and call the police. You can't leave your place unprotected; the front door is unlocked and standing wide open." With that he was roaring down the street in his Jeep. She could hear him shifting gears even as he disappeared into the mist.

The police arrived not long after Tracy called. She told them about the shadowy figure she had seen from her deck and then Shane's encounter with what they believed to be the same person. She could not tell them what kind of car Shane had seen because, in his haste to leave, he hadn't given her a description. Dietrick wrecked his rental and she didn't know what kind he was driving now. She didn't even know if this man was Dietrick.

Everything was going to hell in a hand basket. Nick's disappearance, the attack on Shane, a young man murdered, and now Amy had been abducted—what next? Tracy didn't have a clue why any of this was happening. What started out as an uncomplicated case, or so she thought, had quickly escalated into something very big. Somehow she had to get to the bottom of it all before anyone else was hurt.

After the police left, Tracy wore a trail between the phone and the front window while she waited for news, any news. Gratefully, the fog was beginning to burn off, the only good thing about this whole morning. Hopefully, Shane would now be able to find Amy and bring her back here.

When the phone rang it startled Tracy. As she picked it up, the instrument slipped from her hand and scooted across the floor. She grabbed the handset and pushed the button. "Hello."

"Tracy?"

"Oh, Shane, did you find her?"

"Yes, she managed to get the car door open and jumped out. We're at the hospital."

"What's wrong? Is she injured? How bad is it?"

"Tracy, calm down. We're having her checked over just to make sure, and I took your advice. I got checked, too. They said my head was too hard to receive any damage. Tracy?"

"I'm okay," she answered, brushing away tears of relief, which had suddenly found their way to her eyes. "When will you be back here? Should I come there?"

"The police are with Amy now trying to find out any information that would help them locate your Mr. Dietrick. As soon as they finish we'll be on our way."

"Then it was him?"

"Well, Amy has never seen him but unless there are two elderly men with a German accent interested in you, it was Dietrick, all right." Shane put his hand over the phone and spoke to someone there with him, then came back to her. "Tracy, I have to let you go. The police have some questions for me and we'll be headed your way afterwards."

"Shane, stop by Amy's and have her pack a bag. I think she should stay here with me until this blows over."

"That's a roger. See you shortly."

Tracy put the "closed" sign in the window, locked the door and went upstairs. She had just shut the door when the phone in her private quarters rang. Thinking it might be Nick, she rushed up to her bedroom and quickly answered.

"Hi Tracy."

It was Jean. Tracy bit back disappointment. She had truly hoped Nick was calling. "Hi, Jean. How's it going?"

"Well, probably much better than on your end. Do I detect trouble in your voice?"

Tracy sighed. "You know me too well, my friend. You know I love hearing from you, but Nick is on the missing list and when the phone rang I thought maybe he was found. Not only that, but my manager and friend, Amy, was kidnapped and later escaped. Shane is bringing her here until some of this blows over."

"Is your life ever normal? I doubt any book could be more exciting or adventurous than your life. What happened with Nick?"

"He went to Germany to see if he could find out anything about our Mr. Levine or Dietrick and he didn't come back." Tracy went on to tell her about the last phone call she got from Nick and her call to the hotel. Changing the subject she asked, "How are things going for you?"

"That's the reason I called. I have an interview with a city college in Rockford, Illinois."

"Illinois? It's cold there and so far away. Why there?"

"It's near my mother. She's getting up there in years and I think she needs me now."

"And it's far away from the son-of-a-bitch," Tracy added. "Am I right? Is that what this is really about?"

"Don't be angry, Tracy."

"I'm not angry with you, Jean. I'll miss you, you know that, but I want you to do this for the right reason. Don't uproot your life because of that asshole."

"It's just an interview, I haven't gotten the job yet. Besides, my mom really does need me now. Her health has been failing for the last few months and I worry about her living all alone and so far away. It's that or put her in a home and I just can't do that to her."

"What about your brother? He's closer."

"He has a family, Tracy, and I don't. I have no encumbrances," she said in a choked voice.

"I'm sorry, Jean. I wish you had never gone on that retreat and talked to that woman. When are you going?

"Day after tomorrow."

"Call me when you get back. I don't know if I can wish you luck or not. I'm selfish. I don't know what I'll do without you."

Jean laughed over her tears. "With all the drama in your life? At least you can come visit when you are in the neighborhood visiting Michael."

"That sounds like a plan." Tracy paused and then said, "Keep in touch with me and if you need me for anything don't hesitate to ask."

"I haven't left yet," Jean said. "But I'll hold you to that. I have to go now; there are a lot of things to do. Take care and try to stay out of trouble while I'm gone."

"That's no fun. Have a good trip."

Tracy hung up the phone and went into the other bedroom. She pulled fresh linens from the closet and stripped the bed in the guest room in a frenzy. If she could get her hands on what's-his-name, *Norman,* she would wring his scrawny neck for hurting Jean.

After the bed was made she emptied a couple of drawers in the bureau. Her anger finally quelled, she made one final inspection before going back downstairs to the shop. She wanted to be there when Shane and Amy came back and to see for herself that Amy was okay. The reunion would be bittersweet, though, after the news from Jean.

Getting the room ready kept her mind occupied for a time. Now she needed something else to do. The unfinished inventory sheet still lay on the desk. That would take her full attention and perhaps make the time pass more quickly.

It seemed a short time later when Tracy heard Shane and Amy at the door. She opened it just as Shane was putting the key in the lock.

"Are you all right?" Tracy asked, hugging Amy before holding her away to check her from head to toe.

"Just some scrapes and bruises. I'll be fine. It would have been much worse if he had been traveling faster. Of course the fog slowed him down and then he got a telephone call that seemed to upset him. It had his full attention which made it even easier for me to unlock the door and jump out."

"Wonder what that was all about?"

"I don't know because he didn't say anything, just listened to the voice on the other end. It sure wasn't good news, though."

Chapter Eleven

Nick paced the tiny cell-like room. He could hear muffled voices, but wasn't sure to whom they belonged. Footsteps sounded in the hall, stopping outside the door. Someone turned a key and the door swung open.

"Come with me," the man ordered. He wasn't one Nick had seen before.

Again he was led into the room where Otto was poring over stacks of paperwork on his desk. It seemed an uncanny playback to his arrival here day before yesterday. At least he had been fed and treated decently. He couldn't help wondering if he was being fattened up for the kill, so to speak.

Otto looked up as he entered the room and motioned for him to take a seat. "Mr. Greger, we are going to see to it that you get safely on a plane for America." He got up and went to the filing cabinet, unlocking the top drawer. After retrieving Nick's passport, he handed it to him. "We have made arrangements for tonight's flight at ten thirty."

"What time is it?"

"Four thirty. Now, if you'll go with this gentleman he'll take you where you can shower and get ready."

Aside from the fact these people didn't use names in front of him, except for Otto, Nick was curious about their purpose and wondered why they hadn't asked him more questions.

"Wait. You're finished with me just like that? I didn't tell you where Dietrick—er, Mueller was."

"My colleague has done her research well. We no longer need your assistance. We weren't just interested in answers though, Mr. Greger. As

I stated before, your life is in danger from certain forces in this city. We wanted to be sure you got back to your home safely."

"Who are you people? And is this Mueller fellow one of yours?"

"Who we are is inconsequential, but I can say Mueller is not one of us. The fact is we have been looking for him a very long time and he always stays one step ahead of us. He tortured and murdered many people a long time ago and for this he is a wanted man."

"A Nazi war criminal?" Nick asked incredulously. Alarm shot through his body like a bolt of lightning. "Oh, my God . . . Tracy!"

"We sent a decoy through to the U.S. two days ago in case people here were expecting you at the airport. Tonight, you will also have a decoy to distract any interested parties. And, regrettably, you will have a much longer flight than is ordinary." He handed Nick a bundle topped by a towel, bar of soap and small bottle of shampoo. "My associate will take your clothes when you get in the shower. Just hand them out the door to him." Otto picked up the phone beside him and listened for a moment, then put it back down again. "Mr. Greger, do you know a Tracy Chapman?"

"What about her?"

"She called the hotel looking for you. Unfortunately, I'm afraid the desk clerk had to deny you had ever been in the hotel. It was for your own protection."

"You had no right— "

No-name took Nick by the arm and led him from the room before he could finish. "You'll be able to contact her soon. Right now your safety is top priority."

On the way to the airport, Nick rode in a beat up Volkswagen with one of the no-names while another, dressed in Nick's clothes, went ahead in a sedan that had darkened windows. Once there, Nick and his companion went straight to the check-in counter just as a very noisy commotion broke out a few yards away.

"Wonder what's going on over there?"

"I think there was a Mick Jagger sighting." Nick's companion grinned and winked.

The check-in went smoothly and they boarded the plane ahead of the first class passengers. Mr. No-Name directed him to a window seat and he sat down beside Nick.

"I'll be leaving you in Vienna. From there you'll go to Paris where a friend of mine will meet you. He'll be carrying a sign that reads 'Mr. Charles Champion'. You will go with him where he will put you on another plane, then on to New York. Keep a watchful eye and stay safe."

As the passengers began filling the airplane, Mr. No-Name took out an eye mask and made himself comfortable for the flight. He made it very clear there would be no further conversation.

Nick watched the passengers boarding the plane, making a mental note of their demeanor; it was an occupational practice more than curiosity. Once they were seated and the plane airborne, his thoughts turned to Tracy. He wished he could've called and warned her who she was up against. He had a lot of confidence in her ability to take care of herself and, of course, Shane was there, but this was no ordinary hoodlum with whom they were dealing. True, he was an old man, but an exceptional old man who had accomplices of undetermined talent.

Chapter Twelve

"I took advantage of my contacts and found out that your Mr. Dietrick has disappeared into thin air. He hasn't been back to his motel and he left the rental car parked downtown." Shane tossed his keys onto the table and plopped down in a chair opposite Tracy. "Where's Amy?"

"She's taking a shower." Tracy sat forward and looked at Shane intently. "So, they found out where he was staying? Have they checked to see if he caught the shuttle to the airport?"

"He didn't take the shuttle. Probably thought that would be the first thing we checked. I would think that, if I were him. If he's in town I'm sure they'll find him."

"At least he has more sense than to come around here for a while. Hopefully, I can find out what this is all about before that time comes. I wish Nick would call. I'm really worried about him." Tracy noticed that Shane fidgeted with something in his pocket, but chalked it up to the tension of the last day or two.

"He's a big boy and can take care of himself. As I said, he probably got a hot tip at the last minute and is following it up. I'm sure when he is ready he will call, or just show up. That would be so like him."

The doorbell chimed and both Tracy and Shane were immediately alert. Shane held a finger to his lips and went downstairs. He checked the peek hole and a smile abruptly found its way through the mask of uncertainty. He jerked open the door and wrapped Nick in a bear hug, soundly slapping him on the back.

"Were your ears burning? We were just talking about you."

Nick pushed his friend back inside and cast glances up and down the street before shutting the door. "Lock up and lets go upstairs. I have a lot to tell you guys."

Just as suddenly as Shane's smile appeared, it vanished, wiped away by the ominous tone in Nick's voice. What in the world had happened? What did he find out on this trip that got to the unflappable T. Nicholas Greger?

"Oh, Nick, I'm so glad you're here— " Tracy began, but she stopped in mid-sentence when she noted his mouth was tight and grim.

"I want you to go visit your boyfriend in Montana."

"It's North Dakota and we have been through this before. I have a job to finish."

Nick took her by the shoulders. His dark eyes flashed. In a gentle but firm warning, he said, "This time you have to do as I say. I mean it, Tracy." He let her go and reached over, turned off the lights in the living room, and switched on the hood light over the kitchen range. He moved to the sliding glass door where he cautiously lifted the edge of the drapes and stood peering out at the beach. "This little son-of-a-bitch, forgive my language but that's what he is, who's been terrorizing your life lately is a Nazi war criminal. A very dangerous one, I might add. And that's not all, he has friends still around that are probably every bit as nasty as he is."

He didn't miss the gaze Shane and Tracy exchanged. "What? What have you two done now?" His hand slid beneath his jacket as a sound from the hall interrupted him.

"Why are the lights off?" Amy asked, vigorously rubbing her hair with a towel. She stopped short and pulled the robe belt tighter around her. "Oh, Shane, I didn't know— Nick, when did you— " Her question hung in the air unfinished as she immediately noted the tension that filled the room.

"Amy, what are you doing here? And does this have anything to do with whatever they haven't told me yet?" Nick's glance took in Tracy, then Shane, and back to Amy. "Out with it."

Shane and Tracy started at the same time, and then Tracy gave the floor to Shane. He knew more about what happened than she did and would be more detailed.

"See, that's what I mean. The call was probably from his friends in Germany telling him someone was asking around about him. Hopefully he will slip up and finally face the music. In the meantime, we need to get this settled once and for all and get out of it. Agreed?" When she didn't answer, "Tracy?"

"I just have to go to Nebraska and talk to Hannah and give her the journal. I think she will be able to put the final touch to this case and provide the answers we are lacking."

"*We* will go to Nebraska. You and I are going to be joined at the hip till this thing is over. Amy, do you have relatives you can go visit?"

"I do, but it's not a convenient time for me. I think I'll be safe now. He wouldn't dare try anything again, not with the authorities after him. He has a lot more to lose than your ordinary bad guy." Amy gave a hopeful half-smile and shrugged her shoulders.

"Well, I gotta get some shut-eye. I'm wiped out. Maybe I could crash on your couch for a while, Trace. Amy looks like she is getting ready to go to bed and I think the rest of you should get some sleep, too. Tomorrow we wrap this up. Agreed?"

"I'm with you, Nick." Shane turned to Amy. "Before you go to bed, could I show you something in the shop? It's kinda important. I don't think it can wait."

"Sure." She directed a puzzled look at Tracy and asked, "Is it all right?"

"Of course. Hopefully, you'll be safe in Shane's company." She winked at Shane and he gave her a stern look.

Downstairs, Shane turned and faced Amy. "I have something to ask you and I wanted to do so in private." He pushed stray tendrils of her hair away from her cheek.

"Sure," Amy answered, her eyebrows raised inquiringly.

Shane swallowed hard. "I— I've wanted to ask you this for a while now and I had hoped for a more romantic setting, but with all that's been happening — well, I don't want to put it off any longer. Will you marry me?" He took a small box from his pocket and opened it. A modest diamond solitaire ring twinkled from the black velvet lining.

The heavy lashes that shadowed her cheeks flew up in surprise. She was barely able to control her gasp of surprise. She looked at Shane and back down at the ring.

"Well?" Shane asked. A flicker of disappointment appeared in his eyes as Amy stared speechless at the velvet box he held.

"I don't know what to say."

"Yes will do." His expression stilled and he grew serious.

"Shane, I— we haven't know each other long enough."

"Long enough for me. I knew the moment I saw you that I was going to marry you and maybe it will take a little longer for you. I'm willing to wait as long as it takes."

Amy put her arms around Shane's middle and hugged him. "I'll hold you to that," she murmured against his chest.

"What's with those two?" Nick craned his neck, trying to hear what was going on below.

"That's none of your business."

"Spoil sport." He started to say something else but Amy appeared at the door. "Shane said to tell you guys goodnight, he'll see you in the morning. I think I'll hit the sack, too, if you guys don't mind."

Nick's eyebrows raised inquiringly as he watched Amy walk down the hall and into the bedroom. He didn't miss the tears slipping down her cheeks.

"I think it has something to do with love."

"I'll be damned. How long has this been going on?"

"I think it began when you brought him here, but neither of them recognized it right away." Tracy glanced down the hallway. She wanted to go to Amy and comfort her, but decided against it. When Amy was ready, Tracy would be there. For now, though, she respected her need for privacy.

The next morning Nick left Tracy at the new shop with Amy and Shane and went to the police department to report what he had found out about Dietrick. The shop was coming along nicely. The staging had been completed, prices tucked inconspicuously behind each item and possible hazards eliminated.

Amy and Shane were privately dealing with the new direction their relationship had taken. At the same time, they tried to keep focused on their respective jobs. Tracy could only watch with the hope that the problem would soon be solved, whatever it might be.

Nick was still at the police department when Tracy finished with the last minute details. She wanted to go home and prepare for her trip to see Hannah and she didn't feel the need to wait for him. Since everybody had his or her own agenda, Tracy headed for home alone.

On the winding road, she was occupied with her thoughts when suddenly a bullet whizzed past her nose and shattered the passenger side window. It came from the black car that just passed her. Tracy's hands gripped the wheel. Here we go again! This time she wasn't going to roll over and play dead. For a minute they played tag as the other driver dropped back alongside her then accelerated. The expensive car had more power and moved ahead of her, but she caught him again. This time she saw the driver. "You're too old to be driving like this!" she shouted, "You're going to get yourself killed." He continued his attack. Either he didn't understand or was ignoring her.

A car came around the curve toward them. She had to speed up to get around Dietrick and back in the proper lane. After the car passed, Dietrick pulled alongside her and raised his gun, but lowered it to fight the wheel to keep from going over the edge of the cliff. He gained control of his car and dropped back even with Tracy. He brought the gun up again, aiming it directly at her.

Tracy dropped back and nosed her vehicle toward Dietrick's, catching his back fender and sending it into a fishtail. She could see the old man fighting the wheel. Dietrick was all over the road, his brakes squealing and smoke pouring from his tires before his car plunged through the guardrail and over the cliff. Tracy slammed on her brakes and pulled safely off the road. She tumbled out of the car just in time to see a ball of flame shoot skyward.

Cautiously Tracy peered over the cliff. No way could anyone have survived that, but she was going to make sure. She called 911 and stayed put until the emergency team arrived.

"You call this in?" The paramedic asked after he climbed back up to the highway.

"Yeah. How's it look?"

"He didn't make it."

"I didn't think he did."

"Stick around. You'll need to give a statement to the deputy over there."

Tracy walked over to the edge and looked down. "That's your introduction to hell, old man. You're finally where you belong."

"What's that?" the deputy asked as he approached Tracy.

"Hellava way to go, I was saying."

"Tracy by God Chapman. What in the hell— You could've been killed."

"Oh, hi, Nick."

"Don't." He grabbed Tracy and held her for a minute.

"I told you I could take care of myself. By the way, how did you find out about this?"

"I was at the station when the call came through. Remember, that's where I went thinking you would stay put for a while."

"At least it's over."

"I wouldn't count on it, Tracy." His brows drew downward in a frown. "Whatever he wanted was so important he risked coming out of hiding. He has friends out there still."

"And you think that, given all the notoriety, they will chance coming out of the woodwork?"

"Until you meet with Mr. Levine's family and get rid of his personal effects, this won't be over."

Chapter Thirteen

"Hannah— Mrs. Strasberg?"

"No, this is Sarah, her daughter. Is there something I can help you with?"

Tracy introduced herself and explained why she was there. "I would like to come see your mother and talk to her about her father's arrangements. There is some of his personal property to dispose of, and I have a journal he kept that I would like to give her."

"I don't understand. Her father died over forty-four years ago and he is buried here in Nebraska." Sarah's tone had become chilly. "What kind of joke is this? What is it you want from us?"

"Sarah, the man you know as your grandfather was Hannah's adopted father," Tracy began. "Has she ever talked about her time in Germany before she came to the States?"

"No. I got the idea that was a forbidden subject."

"It was quite an interesting, but dangerous time for your mother and her family. A lot of it is documented in the journal Samuel kept. He wanted his daughter to have it. He had letters in there as well."

"But how can you be certain my mother is the woman you are looking for?"

"I'm pretty sure, but I need to talk to her and see if she remembers Samuel and what happened. Maybe you could tell her I'm here and would like to talk to her." Tracy didn't want to leave the door open for rejection but on the other hand, she didn't want to give the woman a stroke or heart attack by just showing up.

"I'll see. Let me have your phone number."

Tracy gave her the name of the motel where she was staying and the phone number.

"I'll be in touch." Sarah ended the conversation without giving Tracy much hope. Her mother's health was probably uppermost in her mind and Tracy couldn't fault her with that.

The next morning Tracy was jarred awake by the phone. She mumbled into her pillow and pulled the covers over her head. She couldn't remember leaving a wake-up call.

"Hullo," she answered, still groggy from sleep.

"This is the front desk. You have a visitor."

"Who is it?"

Tracy could hear the man talking to someone. When he came back on the phone, he announced, "Mrs. Sarah Adams."

"Sarah?" then, "Would you please ask her to wait in the coffee shop and tell her I'll be right there." Tracy threw the covers back and hurriedly dressed, running a brush through her hair just before she went out the door.

Tracy waited at the "wait to be seated" sign for the hostess. Her gaze swept the crowded room, trying to pick out Sarah. The aroma of breakfast food filled the air, causing Tracy's stomach to rumble and she impatiently tapped her fingers on the sign. Finally, a waitress looked up and noticed her. She grabbed a menu and headed in Tracy's direction.

"Just one in your party?"

"Actually, I'm joining someone. I'm not sure what she looks like."

"There is a Mrs. Sarah Adams expecting someone. Is that the person you're looking for?"

"Yes, that would be the one. Thanks"

The waitress led Tracy to a table where a middle-aged woman sat, her back to Tracy, sipping a cup of coffee. She looked up as Tracy came around the table and hastily set her cup down with a dull clunk against the saucer.

"You must be Sarah?"

Sarah nodded, extending her hand. "And you are Tracy?"

Tracy took the menu and asked the waitress to bring some coffee, then turned her attention back to Sarah.

"Tracy, I decided to come and see what you have before I put too much pressure on my mother."

"Then she isn't going to see me?"

"Well, I can't say right now. I can say, though, you have peaked my curiosity and since you have come such a distance— well, I decided you deserve a chance to tell your story to someone."

"Do you read German?"

"A little, why?"

"The journal is in German."

"Why don't you show me what you have?"

"It's in my room. I wasn't expecting you and when they called and said you were here, I'm afraid I just hurried out without it. I didn't want to keep you waiting."

"I'm sorry. It was rude of me to just show up like this, but I dropped my mother at the senior center, and, since I was in the neighborhood, I decided to stop by." Sarah looked up as the waitress brought another cup for Tracy, filled it and set the carafe in the middle of the table. "We talked a little last night, but she wasn't very receptive," she continued. "Tell me about this Samuel Levine who might be my grandfather."

"Well, I'm afraid I never met him, but through his journal I have come to respect and admire him for his courage and fortitude." Tracy picked up the cup of coffee and sipped the hot liquid gingerly. "I have a friend who speaks German fluently and I asked her to translate the journal for me. I was hoping it would contain information that would lead me to his family. I think it has."

"May I see it?"

"If you don't mind, rather than me bringing it here, we can go back to my room, where it is more private." Tracy signed the bill, writing her room number on it.

"That will be fine."

Sarah paled when Tracy showed her the photographs. "You've seen these before?"

"Well, not these particular photographs, but one taken of my mother when she was about this same age." Sarah carefully ran her finger over the faces in the photograph. "There is such a resemblance. My son looks so much like the man there."

"Samuel Levine is his name and that's his wife, Esther. The little girl's name is Hannah."

Sarah looked at the photo for several minutes. "It seemed they were so happy here. How sad so much evil tore at their lives, and so many thousands more. I can't even begin to fathom." She set the photograph on the bed and opened the journal. Slowly she read the pages while Tracy made coffee in the room's small coffee pot. When Tracy offered a cup, Sarah silently waved her off and continued to read.

When she had finished, Sarah set the journal down beside the photographs. Tears filled her eyes and slipped down her cheeks. Tracy grabbed several tissues and offered them to her.

"It's very moving isn't it? My friend and I kinda had the same reaction."

"Thanks," Sarah said as she took the tissues. "The thing is, I really think this is my grandfather. The family resemblance, the names of the family who adopted my mother— " Sarah wiped her eyes and discreetly blew her nose. A few moments passed before she spoke again. "My mother has mentioned being in Lyon, but she won't talk about what happened before that. I think it was forbidden for so long, she may have blocked some of it from her mind."

"Do you think her health is such this might be harmful to her?"

"No, I don't think so. She's a pretty sturdy old gal, my mother, but she is also very stubborn and therein lies the problem— getting her to talk about all this."

"Why don't you take the photographs and show them to her? Tell her what you found out and see if she will talk to me," Tracy suggested, but opted not to offer the journal. She preferred to keep it in her possession until the time she could personally give it to Hannah.

"I can't promise you anything."

"Just give it all you've got." Hesitantly, Tracy handed her the photographs. She had been guarding them so reverently. They had been part of the journey she had taken with Samuel through his journal entries; putting a face to the man whose adventures she shared. "You will be careful with these, won't you?" *Just in case you aren't the right family*, she wanted to add.

Sarah reached over and touched Tracy's hand gently. "You know I will. I am moved by your concern for these and your dedication in finding the family they belong to. I'll be in touch. Thank you so much."

Tracy gave Sarah a hug at the door and watched as she walked to her car. She was hopeful she could close the door on this case and give Samuel back to his family. It had been a long time coming and it had taken a long two and a half weeks to find them.

Twenty-four hours passed before Sarah called again. When the phone rang, Tracy grabbed it before the second ring.

"Tracy, this is Sarah. My mother would like for you to come over this afternoon and have lunch with us."

"Then she will see me? Good job, Sarah. What time should I be there?"

"Around noon, if that's convenient for you. Shall I come by and pick you up?"

"No, I have a rental and I took the liberty of printing out a map to your place when I first got here. I think I can manage. If I get lost I'll give you a call."

"Then noon it is."

Tracy hung up the phone and excitedly thrust two thumbs in the air. "Yes!" Finally, she could give Hannah back her father after all these years. Unfortunately, her excitement was short-lived because she thought of the events at home. She would try to put that in the back of her mind for the time being. Too much was riding on the visit with Hannah. She didn't want any distractions to keep her from giving Hannah her past. Most of all she didn't want to mess up this meeting.

Tracy drove through downtown Hastings. It was a small business district and very clean. There were statues on the sidewalks and she slowed down to catch a glimpse of some. One featured two young boys with their arms around each other. One held a bat and the other a basketball. Both had perpetual smiles upon their faces. A little farther down was a tribute to the American farmer in his overalls and striking a "Thinker" pose.

Another statue that caught Tracy's attention was of a young boy sitting on a bench, one leg crossed over the other with a large book in his lap. There were others she wanted to see, but the traffic got heavy since it was around the noon hour and she was expected at Hannah's. What a delight, she thought and she was pleased she had taken this route.

Having found Twelfth Street, Tracy turned onto it. She drove slowly, watching the numbers. The address belonged to a craftsman-style, two-story house with well-kept lawn and gardens. A raised front porch in the front ran the width of the house and four brick pillars supported white columns. In between each of these columns were white contoured t-rail railings supported by square pickets, or columns. A porch swing hung just behind the railing and to the side of a large three paneled picture window.

Her stomach was doing flip-flops, forcing her to take deep, calming breaths. Success in this venture mattered to her more than she had realized. Tracy sat in the car for a moment summoning the strength to face the coming encounter that could result in success or in failure.

The front door opened and Sarah stepped out onto the porch. When Tracy didn't get out, she bent over and looked down the sloping yard to see what was taking so long. Finally, she caught Tracy's attention and motioned for her to come on in.

Smiling, Tracy waved and shut off the engine. She gathered up the journal and her briefcase, and stuffed her phone into her purse, which she slipped over her arm. "Well, Tracy ole girl this is it." A deep sigh escaped her lips as she opened the car door and hurried up the walk.

Sarah gave her a quick hug and held the glass-fronted storm door open. Just inside, Tracy stopped to admire the wooden door with beveled glass panes leading into the house from the enclosed summer porch. Sarah smiled, acknowledging her appreciation. She took Tracy's arm and directed her into the front parlor where an elderly woman sat in a much worn recliner. As her eyes met Tracy's, a nervous smile tugged at her mouth.

"Miss Hannah," Tracy acknowledged and crossed the room. When the woman started to get up Tracy stopped her with a raised hand. "Please don't get up. I'll just prop here beside you." She eased down on the raised stone hearth and stretched her legs out in front of her, placing her purse and briefcase on the floor.

"Let me bring a chair over for you," Sarah offered, "that rock can get pretty hard after a while."

"I'll be fine, really. Thanks, Sarah." Tracy watched as Sarah left the room, hoping to find the words to begin the conversation with Hannah. She still held the journal and noticed that the elderly woman was staring intently at the book.

"Is that it?" Hannah asked. "Is that the journal my Sarah spoke of?"

"Yes," Tracy answered simply and handed her the journal. Her mouth was suddenly dry and she couldn't say anything more.

"The picture you gave Sarah, the one of the woman and little girl, that was my mother and I, and the other one was taken with my father before— " Hannah lifted a wrinkled hand to her throat and let it lie there before she spoke again. Her eyelids fluttered fighting back tears and for a minute Tracy worried that the memory was too much for her. "I didn't want to meet you at first, to know if this Samuel Levine was indeed my father. I became very angry." She looked away and was quiet for a time.

"Angry? I don't understand."

"That time so long ago. It was a tragic time for me, for a lot of people. After we left home we waited to hear from my father and when there was no word, we feared the worst. We heard the bad things that were happening in Germany, to my people and— well, my mother became very ill. I think it was because she feared my father had been killed, possibly even tortured before he died. She just didn't have the heart to go on. I can look back now and see— " Hannah wiped her eyes with a delicate lace-bordered handkerchief. "The horror of that time, of losing both my parents and being taken away by strangers to a new country; it was all too much for my young mind to bear. I'm afraid I pushed all those memories to a deep, dark corner of my mind."

Sarah entered the room quietly carrying a glass of lemonade. Tracy took the glass and whispered thanks to Sarah before returning her gaze to Hannah.

"After my Papa died, my adopted Papa, I ran across a lot of papers and newspaper clippings from that time and those memories started to come back, but they were incomplete. I never spoke of them. When Sarah told me that you had news of a man who might be my father, I first wouldn't believe it. My father had died all those years ago in Germany. If he hadn't, then why didn't he join my mother and me as he promised? Why did he let her die believing he was dead? Why did he let strangers take me away?" Hannah bowed her head, taking a deep breath and once again a hand went to her throat.

Tracy reached out and took the woman's other hand and held it. "Are you okay with this? I mean— "

"Am I going to have a stroke or something?" Hannah smiled through the tears. "No, dear, I'm healthy as an ox, for an old woman." She lifted some papers on the table beside her and pulled out the two pictures Tracy sent with Sarah. "All those questions you raised by coming here are the reason I grew angry, but then, by the same token, they raised my curiosity."

"I can tell you that your father did come to France for you but you were already gone. He also went to South Dakota looking for you."

"Why did he wait so long?" She asked tearfully.

"To learn that, you will need to read the journal he left for you."

Hannah once again ran her fingers over the book. She sat staring at it for a time until Tracy spoke again. "Read it, Miss Hannah. All the answers to those questions are right there in that book. Sarah and I will give you some privacy." Tracy stood and prepared to leave when she remembered the poem at the end of the journal. "Miss Hannah, there is a poem of sorts at the end and it's rather cryptic, unlike the rest of your father's writing. Maybe you can shed some light on that."

Hannah turned to the entry in question. "Ah, it is a puzzle. My father used to write many of these to see if I could unlock the meaning. He said it would sharpen my wit and increase my brain-power." She smiled sadly at the memory and shook her head. "When I've read this book I will see if I can solve the mystery. It's been a lifetime ago."

Tracy wasn't sure if she should return to her motel and give Hannah privacy to read the journal, or stay. Sarah provided an answer to her dilemma.

"Would you like to see the rest of the house? I noticed you have an appreciation of older things."

"That would be great. As for the appreciation of older things, that is my business as well as a hobby. I have an antique shop back in California."

When they were out of hearing range Sarah confided, "My mother hasn't been at her best since she saw the pictures. I wasn't sure if she should be subjected to this stress after all, but she was adamant about seeing the journal."

"I would think she is entitled to the information about her father and what happened to him, and also to put him at rest while she still has the time. Her father deserves that much after all he went through."

They came to more wooden doors; these were double, filled with the same beveled glass panes and led into the dining room. A built-in china cabinet trimmed in the same dark wood filled the wall on one side of the room. The cabinet had two rows of glass-fronted doors atop a lower chest with drawers and smaller doors. A crystal chandelier hung from the ceiling. Along the far side of the wall, a leaded window looked out onto the summer porch, while the same type of door as the others led out to the back yard.

Just to the left, before entering the kitchen, three steps accompanied by a beautifully carved banister, climbed to another set of double doors. These were solid and when opened revealed a staircase to the upper floor.

A floor-to-ceiling spice rack was attached to the dark cabinets as Tracy entered the spacious kitchen. There was an abundance of counter space and storage. A large window above the sink looked out into the English-style gardens in the back yard.

Sarah led Tracy outside where a white picket fence wrapped around a garden in which peonies, poppies and irises bloomed amidst assorted greenery. Trees provided a dark, cool shade and almost hid several outbuildings in various stages of decline.

They went around to the front porch and were about to sit in the swing, when they noticed Hannah standing in the sun porch doorway. She motioned for them to come back inside.

"Sarah, Miss Chapman," Hannah called in a weak voice. She leaned against the door's frame for support, her head bowed.

"Mom!" Sarah's voice cracked with fear as she ran towards her mother, Tracy following closely behind her.

Chapter Fourteen

Sarah helped her mother back to her chair. "Should I call Dr. Goldman? Is it your heart? Oh, my God, I shouldn't have let you do this."

Hannah waved a hand, dismissing her daughter's concern. "I'm all right, Sarah. It's just that all the sadness has weakened me. Sit down, both of you." Hannah wiped her tears and picked up the journal again. "I have to think about this poem a little more. I'm not sure I can figure it out. This old brain has many cobwebs and dark corners where my memory hides."

"Perhaps I can come back tomorrow, after you've had some rest and lived with the poem a while." Tracy felt a veil of disappointment drop around her and she tried to make her voice sound more optimistic than she felt. Maybe she shouldn't have pressed Hannah to read the journal; she had finished her job, having found Samuel's daughter. After all, she was only supposed to find family members so they could take possession of the remains.

There still are unanswered questions, though. What was Dietrick looking for? Was it something in the journal, or something yet to be discovered in Samuel's belongings? Did the poem contain only fatherly advice, or was it hiding a warning of some sort? Tracy wanted to find the answers before she left Hastings.

"Well, let's just have another look."

"Are you sure you're all right? I would hate to know all this was too stressful for you."

"I'm okay, really I am. Old age robs one of many things, my dear, as you will surely find out one day." Hannah smiled wearily at Tracy. "Sarah, why don't you bring in some Kool-Aid?" Hannah grinned and winked at her daughter. "Kool- Aid was invented here in Hastings," she explained. "I'll try again to see if I can tell you about the poem, then we can have lunch. My father was definitely trying to tell me something.

"If you don't mind, I'd like to help. Could you read the poem aloud to me in English and slowly?" Tracy asked.

Hannah nodded and picked up the journal. She placed her glasses on her nose and began to read:

"My darling daughter,
I share with you some thoughts I've gained through the years:
Treasure love, but do not love treasure
Much of the first and some of the second
Are the best measure."

"Wait," Tracy interrupted. "If I heard that right, he is telling you to value love more than money, but to value money a little. Is that right?"

"Sounds reasonable."

"Go ahead."

"Love will bind you to him and him to you
But too many riches will bind you both in chains
And together not long will you remain.
Yea, empty pockets breed contempt
And few of us are exempt
From holding those we love to blame
When so little we strive in vain
So, riches are welcome indeed
As we want to fill our daily need."

"That sounds a little contradictory. Now he's saying to welcome money. I don't get it." Tracy slipped an errant strand of hair behind her ear and lines of concentration deepened along her brow and under her eyes.

Hannah continued:

"To understand a man you must go inside
For it is there the mysteries lie.
Beneath the covers one must look

For each of us is like a book.
The jewels of knowledge abound inside
For it is here that truth resides.
And with each reading more is revealed
Until finally we know what's real."

"I agree with him that you can't judge a person just by looking at him. You have to get to know someone to really see them as a whole." Tracy sat silently for a moment analyzing the words. "There seems to be an underlying meaning." She pulled on her lower lip. "It's like he's trying to tell us something."

"What is that underlying message?" Hannah stared at the words. She tapped her forehead gently with three fingers, her smallest resting on the rim of her glasses.

"It seems like he references jewels and treasure a lot within the message to you."

"Of course, that's because he was a jeweler— what?" Hannah's eyebrows rose inquiringly when Tracy suddenly sat forward in her chair.

"Maybe he left you some jewels and the key to finding them is in that poem. I can tell you this, though, I went through all his belongings when I was trying to locate family members and didn't find anything like that."

"Or maybe the journal is the treasure of which he speaks," Sarah added. "It certainly is of historical value and he does mention 'beneath the covers' and 'each of us is like a book'."

"No, I think Tracy is right about the jewels. He was, after all, in the business, and before we left he concealed a lot of the jewelry. I remember Mama had cloth-covered diamonds for buttons on her dress and jewels and money hidden in the hem of her coat and mine. That's what we lived on." She shook her head slowly, amazed at remembering. "Perhaps the book and the treasure are more related than we think. Could it be that the treasure lies within this book itself?"

"That could be what he meant by beneath the covers, otherwise, I think he would have written 'between the covers'," Sarah agreed.

"Maybe there's a map in the book we missed." Hannah held the book up and shook it. "Nothing."

"I think Sarah might be right and it's 'beneath' the covers. It's certainly thick enough." Tracy's measured the book's width with an appraising glance.

Hannah turned to Sarah. "Go and get me that sharp paring knife. There's only one way to find out."

Sarah returned from the kitchen with a knife and hesitantly handed it to her mother. "Maybe we could do it carefully so that the damage could be easily repaired."

With care, Hannah slit the inside binding near the spine of the journal. Once that was released the cover separated from the book and a folded sheet of paper, along with a sparkling diamond necklace, slid out. For a minute, the women were speechless, astonished to see such spectacular jewels.

Hannah picked up the paper and unfolded it. "It's my father's handwriting.

'Dear Hannah, this necklace I made for a German soldier named Karl Mueller under the threat of death. He is a vicious killer and thief. He stole the diamonds from a Jewish gem dealer with whom I did business, until his death at the hands of Herr Mueller. I smuggled it out of Germany after you and my dear Esther left. It didn't belong to Mueller or his kind. This is why I couldn't leave with you and your mother. I was being watched and would have brought Mueller's wrath upon us all had I appeared to be leaving the city.

'I leave it to you as a legacy and hope you will use it wisely. I also hope by the time you get it, the thief will be dead or in prison and no longer in search of it. Surely he will pay for his atrocities someday.

Your loving father'

"Oh my, what in the world are you going to do?" Tracy asked.

"I will probably look at it for a while then give it to the Jewish Relief fund. I have no need for anything like this. My needs are met and I'll leave my family with enough to help them through. This belongs to the Jewish people."

Tracy sat down and stared at the necklace. Samuel had been through so much trying to make enough money to reconnect with his family when all along he carried a fortune. It made his journey even sadder. This was what Dietrick, or Mueller, was after. "This necklace must be worth a fortune! There are twenty three large diamonds here and it looks like they all match."

Suddenly, Tracy's phone rang. She looked at the caller I.D. "I'm sorry, I need to take this call." She stepped out onto the sun porch.

"Hi, Tracy." Nick sounded tired. "How are things going on your end?"

"Great! We've unlocked the puzzle, but I prefer to tell you about it when I return. I have a flight in the morning. I should be there around three in the afternoon."

"Good; I can meet you at the airport. By the way, Shane and Amy send their love. Oh, hell!" The connection was terminated.

Nick threw his cell phone onto the seat. Marcos, the missing hoodlum, drove past him. Nick recognized him from a mug shot he'd seen in police records. He always believed Marcos would return to familiar territory one day. Perhaps Marcos realized jail was a much better place than where his friend ended up, or maybe he just got tired of running.

Nick stepped on the gas. He called the police just as he caught up with Marcos and motioned for him to pull over. When he saw the guy was uncooperative, he pulled his gun and aimed it at him. Marcos eased off the accelerator and parked on the edge of the highway. Nick left his vehicle and leaned against the man's car door, his gun ready, waiting for the police to arrive.

His cell phone chirped again, noting he had a message. Nick knew who called without looking. He also knew he'd better return her call before she flew back without a plane.

"Hi, Tracy. You called?" He grinned as he waited for the storm.

"What happened? I've been frantic trying to reach you. Don't ever do that to me again!"

"Just a pesky problem I had to take care of. Can't talk right now, but I knew you'd wonder what was going on. Just finish up there and I'll fill you in when you come home."

"Does it have anything to do with our friend?"

"A long-lost one." Nick smiled, "Gotta go. There's a man here wanting to talk to me right now. I don't want to keep him waiting."

Tracy closed her cell phone and held it for a moment before putting it away. She thought his answer curious, but at least Nick was okay and she would definitely find out what was going on soon. It was going to be an early dinner, packing, and bed for her. When they were completed, Sarah would fill her in on details of the trip to retrieve her grandfather's remains.

Before Tracy left there was another question still haunting her. She was still curious as to why the relatives had lied to Samuel when he came looking for Hannah. Tracy opened the door and went back into the room. "I have another puzzle to be solved. Why was your father told the Steinfelds had moved to California when he came looking for you? I can understand they wouldn't want to give you up, but it was assumed he had died in Germany."

"I can't say. Perhaps they feared their life was in danger, or that an enemy was looking for them. The Jewish people had many at one time." Hannah shook her head slowly. "I'm afraid they took the answer to the grave with them."

Chapter Fifteen

Tracy checked her watch. Two hours before Sarah's plane would land in San Jose, then another two hours on the shuttle and she would be here in Monet Cove. Sarah would be accompanying her grandfather's remains back to Nebraska, since Hannah's age made her too frail for such a long trip. This chapter of Tracy's life would soon be over and she could move on. In a way, she felt a pang of regret at letting go her connection with the Levine family. She had a lot to do, though, and mentally checked off the list. There were still things in the new store that needed to be made ready before opening for business in less than a month, and there was the trip to South Dakota.

As Tracy stepped from her new shop, she collided with a young girl. Had her responses not been so quick, the girl would have fallen to the sidewalk. Tracy continued to hold on to her until she had regained her balance. Something was wrong.

"Are you all right?" Tracy asked. When there was no answer Tracy took a closer look at the pale, dazed girl. She appeared to be very young, thirteen or fourteen Tracy guessed. Again Tracy asked if she was all right. It was then the girl's eyes rolled back into her head and she collapsed completely.

Keeping a firm grip with one hand, Tracy fished in her handbag for her cell phone, while calling out to anyone who might help, "Call 911, please! Would someone call 911?"

"I got it," a man yelled to her. "They are on their way."

Tracy eased the unconscious girl down onto the sidewalk and made her as comfortable as she could under the circumstances. She patted the girl's face, then her hands, trying to arouse her.

It seemed forever before Tracy heard the siren, but in actuality it was only a couple of minutes. The paramedics moved in and took over and Tracy stood back to let them do their job. Once the girl was in the ambulance, a policeman stepped forward and began questioning Tracy.

"I don't know anything about her or what caused her to pass out. I don't think I bumped into her hard enough to knock her out, at least I hope not."

"I don't see a purse or anything that would contain identification," the officer observed. "Did you see a purse in her possession?"

"I'm afraid I didn't see much of anything, officer. My only thought was for her health and to keep her from falling on the sidewalk. That pretty much took my whole concentration." Tracy watched the ambulance pull away from the curb. "Anything else, officer?"

"No, I think that's it."

Tracy headed for her car, again checking her watch. There would be enough time to go to the hospital and check on the girl. She wanted to make sure she was all right.

Tracy checked in with the emergency room desk, letting them know she was there for the young girl who was just brought in by ambulance and would appreciate any information they could give her, once the doctor had finished his examination. Tracy explained how she was involved.

"Hey, Miss Chapman." It was Officer Harry Foreman.

"Hi Harry," Tracy answered, walking across the lobby to meet him. "I'm glad to see you." She told him about the young girl and expressed interest in her condition. "I don't think I will be able to find out much from the hospital."

"I'll see what I can find out, and I'll fill you in, once I know anything."

"Thanks, I'd appreciate that."

An hour passed, then two. Tracy paced the waiting room floor hoping to hear something soon. Before long she would have to meet the shuttle and take Sarah to the funeral home.

Tracy wanted to let someone know she was leaving, but would be back in touch for information. Officer Foreman was on a coffee run to the cafeteria and the nurse had left her station. She was searching in her purse for something on which to leave a note when Foreman returned.

"I stopped by to check and see if there was anything on her condition yet. They've taken her to intensive care unit, but that is all I could find out right now."

"I have to leave, but I'll check back with you later on. At least she is in good hands for now."

Tracy watched as the passengers got off the shuttle. Sarah was one of the last to exit and when she spotted Tracy, she smiled and waved.

"How was the flight?" Tracy asked, relieving Sarah of her luggage.

"Great. Smooth ride almost the whole way. The layover in Denver was long, but I walked around the terminal quite a bit."

"We'll stop by the hotel. Then you have an appointment at the funeral home to make the arrangements. After that, I'll drop you off at the hotel. You'll have a chance to freshen up and I'll pick you up later for dinner. How does that sound?"

"You don't have to do all that. I'm sure you're a very busy person."

"Nonsense, I want to." Tracy nodded in the direction of her car and switched the luggage into her other hand. She unlocked the hatch and stowed it away.

"Our rabbi was in touch with a rabbi here and he saw to the preparation of my grandfather's body, but I need to see his possessions if that's okay. We will need his *talit* for burial and if he has a *kipah* as well." Sarah laughed when she saw the blank look Tracy offered her. "The *talit* is the skull cap and the *kipah* a prayer shawl. A Jewish male is usually buried wearing them."

"We can swing by the warehouse. All his clothes and personal belongings are there."

Within ten minutes Tracy pulled into the warehouse parking lot. She walked to the door, pulling the keys from her purse. Once inside she took Sarah to the back of the building and pointed to a section in the corner.

"Some of his clothes are in the drawers beneath that desk over there and his other clothes are packed in those see through containers."

"He was a frugal man, wasn't he?"

"Yes. I was surprised to see he had no family mementoes and had acquired very few personal effects in his eighteen years here. Perhaps he never gave up hope of finding you and wanted to be able to leave at a moment's notice."

At the hotel, Sarah checked in and they found their way through the maze of hallways. Opening the door to her room, she and Tracy gave it a close inspection.

"Everything looks— " Tracy began, but was interrupted by her cell phone.

"This is Tracy." She paused and continued in sinking tones, "How very sad. Does anyone know what happened to her before she collapsed in my arms? Oh. Oh, God. Please keep me posted."

"Bad news?" Sarah asked.

Tracy told her about the young girl's collapse earlier then related the news she just received. "It seems she had recently given birth— probably even this morning— and apparently without the benefit of a doctor. She died from complications. She was only fourteen years old. The officer didn't go into many details because he has a lot to do right now. They are going to try and backtrack her movements for the day and see if they can find the baby. They aren't sure if they will be able to, or even if it is still alive."

"Let's skip dinner then and I can take a cab to the funeral home. I'm sure you will be tied up with all that's going on."

"No, I could use the company. Besides there is not much I can do at this point but wait to hear what else comes of this." Tracy was about to put her phone away when it rang again.

"Father Kennedy just called from Saint Anne's Cathedral. He said a baby had been found among the pews." Although there was a lot of commotion in the background, it was excitement that increased the volume of Foreman's voice.

"I'm so glad she had the courage to make sure her baby was safe. Too often we hear on the news about mothers killing their babies, especially those mothers so young," An equally excited Tracy said. "Was there anything with the baby that could lead to the mother's identity?"

"There was a note telling them she couldn't take care of the baby and she knew Alicia would be safe at the church. That's what the note said. The child's name is Alicia," Foreman covered the phone with his hand and spoke to someone with him, then he was back. "As yet the department hasn't processed the scene. I'll fill you in when we get the information."

Someone near him once again summoned Foreman and he hurriedly finished his conversation with Tracy. "Before I go I wanted to tell you that Marcos spilled his guts. He and Jack Holgate were working for Dietrick. When they proved to be incompetent, Dietrick killed Jack and had Marcos help him get rid of the body. Marcos knew he was next and he skipped out as soon as the body was dumped."

"Thanks, Harry, I guess I kinda knew that all along." Tracy disconnected the call and turned to Sarah. "I'll wait in the lobby while you freshen up. I noticed they had coffee and some comfortable looking chairs there. Don't hurry."

The paperwork at the funeral home took longer than either Tracy or Sarah thought it would. It was late by the time they had dinner and returned to the hotel.

"Well, Sarah, I am pleased to have been a part of this, however sad the occasion. At least your family was made whole again and I acquired new friends. Tell your mother hello for me when you get back, and thanks for allowing me to have the desk. I think I will keep that piece to remember Mr. Levine's journey and your family." Tracy gave Sarah a hug and started for her car. "What time is the shuttle picking you up in the morning?"

"Five o'clock. Ugh!" Sarah's smile faded and her expression grew serious. "Let me know how things turn out with the baby and if the police find out her mother's identity. How sad it will never know it's mother."

"I will. Good night, and have a safe trip." Tracy watched Sarah walk into the lobby of the hotel. Then Sarah turned back and waved. Tracy felt a tug at her heart thinking of the sad trip ahead for her and maybe a little sadness at saying goodbye to her Samuel and to his daughter and granddaughter.

The next morning Tracy went to her warehouse to meet Vinnie and Harry, who were going to move Samuel's desk to her house. Amy would let them in and show them where she wanted the desk placed. Once they had it loaded, Tracy would go to her kickboxing tournament.

The butterflies were very active in her stomach and she tried not to think of the tournament. She wanted so badly to win this time. Lately there had been no time for practice sessions, but she was determined to give it everything she had.

Tracy watched Vinnie nose the truck into traffic, before she headed for her car. The right front tire was flat. "Damn! Now what?" Tracy took out her cell phone to call Amy.

"On a hot trail, Chapman?"

"Oh, sorry. I didn't see you, Garth." She glanced up at him, her finger poised above the keypad on her phone.

"Need some help?"

"What? Oh, yes. I guess I was just preoccupied with my tournament. I'm going to be late. What brings you to this side of town?"

"As a matter of fact, you do. I have something I'd like to discuss with you. That is, if you have a moment. I can drop you off and we can discuss business on the way."

"Well— " Tracy checked her watch. She would barely get there in time if Garth dropped her off, but if she waited for her tire to be changed she might not make it at all.

"I'm parked out on the street." Garth stopped and inhaled deeply. "You're not afraid to be alone with me, are you Chapman?" He gave a wicked little laugh.

"Now why would you think that? Do you have ulterior motives?" Tracy grabbed her gym bag and followed him to his car.

Again he laughed as he closed the passenger door and hurried to the driver's side of the vehicle. Garth glanced around before folding his six feet plus frame behind the wheel. He checked the side-view mirror as he pulled out into the stream of traffic.

"Okay, what is this all about?"

"All in good time, Chapman." Garth stepped on the accelerator and glanced sideways at Tracy. "What's new with your assignment?"

"It's— hey, you just passed the gym. Turn at the next street and go in behind— " Tracy glanced over her shoulder as they passed the street.

He gave her a sidelong glance. A shadow of annoyance crossed his face and his brows moved together in an angry frown, but Garth made no attempt to slow down. "I'm afraid you're going to miss your tournament after all."

"Where are you taking me and what is this about?" In spite of her reserve, a tinge of exasperation came into her voice.

"Just outside of town where we can have a quiet, undisturbed conversation." He cast a sideways glance at her again. "Patience, Chapman."

"I'm not going anywhere else with you. Pull over right now and let me out or I'll— "

"You'll what?" He cast a sideways glance at her. "Behave yourself if you want to see that little shopkeeper of yours again."

"Amy? You have Amy?"

"Just co-operate with me and no harm will come to her." Garth's mouth spread into a thin-lipped smile.

"You rotten son of a bitch."

"Chapman, really. Is that any way for a lady to talk?" His voice hardened ruthlessly. "Don't give me any trouble. I meant what I said."

Fear and anger knotted within her. She was confident she could handle herself in this situation, but now she had to think of Amy's safety. *Just play along,* she thought, *he'll slip up given the opportunity; and I'll certainly give him that opportunity.*

As Garth promised, they drove a short distance outside of town and turned into a driveway or private road, Tracy wasn't sure which. He jumped out and opened the gate.

"Pull the car on through," Garth instructed.

"Are you sure you trust me?"

"I'm sure you wouldn't do anything to put Amy in jeopardy."

Tracy moved over to the driver's side. Her foot hovered over the accelerator. For a minute she was tempted to ram the car into Garth, but she had to think of Amy. If she killed Garth, which she wanted to do, Amy's whereabouts would remain unknown to her. Instead, she eased the car forward, put the gear in Park and scooted back to the passenger seat. Garth closed the gate behind the vehicle and jumped back inside.

The dirt road snaked through groves of manzanita and cedar trees and climbed up a sharp incline, where a small cabin sat encircled by shrubs and more cedar trees. Its wooden exterior, a faded grey-green color, gave it an air of invisibility against the surrounding woods.

"Here we are," he stated.

"Is Amy here?"

"No," he said simply and walked to the cabin door. He reached above it and retrieved a key, then looked over his shoulder at her.

Tracy stepped from the vehicle and held on to the corner of the car door. She surveyed the area and a shadow of alarm touched her face. "Where is she?"

"Are you going to just stand there, Chapman?" he asked, avoiding her question. "You'll be much more comfortable in here." When she didn't move, Garth walked over and took her by the arm. "I told you you'd be more comfortable inside. You'd do well to start listening to me." His voice was more forceful and his fingers dug into the soft flesh of her upper arm.

It was obvious the cabin had been closed up for some time because stale odors slipped through the open door to greet them. Inside, dust covers sheathed the furniture creating a ghostly appearance in the dark room. Garth closed the door behind him and switched on the overhead light. He led Tracy to the sofa and forced her to sit down.

As casually as she could manage she asked, "What's this about, Garth?"

"You have control of something very valuable. Something I want." Garth sat down in a chair opposite her. "For years you have been there ahead of me and gotten the best items, leaving me the scraps. Well, things are about to turn in my favor."

"I don't understand. You've had just as much of an opportunity as I have, Garth, and you've done quite well. Your shop is every bit as good as mine."

"Shop. Not two shops, just one. And you skipped right over the important part. That's so like you." His gaze was dark and troubled. "There was an item worth millions in the personal effects of Mr. Samuel Levine. I bet you didn't know I was aware of it."

"I'm afraid I don't know what you're talking about. You saw the furniture. You even looked through the one piece that was of any value— the antique desk."

Garth stood and began to pace. "I'm losing my patience with you. You know what I'm talking about and I want to know where it is."

"Where what is?"

"Don't be crass, Chapman. The item is a necklace that belonged to my client. In fact, I was promised a fortune if I returned it to him. He's dead. You killed him before I had a chance to collect, and now I fully intend to have the whole deal."

Tracy was caught off guard. No one knew about the necklace but she and the Levine family. No one else, except Dietrick, or Mueller as they had found out was his true name. Of course, Jack Holgate probably knew, but he was dead. His sidekick was in jail, but Tracy was pretty certain he was not the client either. "And was your client one Karl Mueller?"

"No, his name was Rutger Dietrick."

"One and the same. Unfortunately, he was not the true owner." As casually as she could manage, Tracy asked, "How did you two happen to hook up?"

"Dietrick came into my shop and looked over my merchandise. He asked me if I had gotten anything else in the past week or so that might not be on display yet. He seemed to be at wits end. So, when I asked what he was looking for, it took me a while to gain his trust, but he finally told me about his necklace. He said he thought it was in your possession, but was checking with me just in case. After a few more minutes he told me about the fiasco created by the young hoodlums he hired, and he offered me the deal and I accepted. End of story." He paced the room as he talked, his expression one of pained tolerance.

Garth stopped in front of Tracy and bent down, taking her by the shoulders. His lips thinned with irritation and he gave her a little shake. "Where is the necklace?"

"I don't have it."

"I caution you, Chapman, you are not in a position to be evasive. Now, I repeat, where is that necklace?"

"With its rightful owner."

His fingers dug into her shoulders and he gave her a murderous look. "Not the right answer. I know it hasn't surfaced, because that news would be the talk of the day. What the hell, it would be the talk of the year. Now, where is that necklace?"

"What I want to know is why Dietrick would tell you exactly what he was looking for?" Tracy still didn't understand why Dietrick would confide in anyone else, and especially Garth, about the necklace. She was almost sure he hadn't revealed how he acquired the jewels. Even Garth wouldn't agree to a deal based on murder and thievery, or would he? Kidnapping wasn't something she believed him capable of either, and now he had kidnapped two people.

"You mean, as opposed to the thugs he hired before? He knew I could be trusted because I am a businessman and an expert in the field. Why shouldn't he trust me?"

"The other question I have is why would an honest businessman suddenly turn into a kidnapper and murderer?"

"I haven't murdered anyone!"

"How do I know you haven't killed Amy? And do you really think I believe you will release me so I can go straight to the police?"

"Tsk, tsk, Chapman, I wouldn't harm you, maybe I'll hurt Amy if you don't co-operate. I just plan on detaining you and your friend long enough to acquire the necklace and then get out of the country."

"Where is Amy?"

"In a safe place for now. I can't guarantee that to be the case if you give me any trouble."

"You'd ruin your reputation, leave your home and business, for what? A few million dollars? And when the money runs out, then what? You can't come home again."

Garth ran his fingers through his hair in a nervous gesture. He momentarily seemed to struggle with an inner torment. "I'm a dead man either way.

Chapter Sixteen

Nick paced outside the gym, glancing at his watch. Tracy should have been here thirty minutes ago. He dialed her cell phone number again but still there was no answer. He went back inside and found Shane.

"Anything?" Nick mouthed, knowing he would never be heard above the noise in the gym.

Shane shook his head and motioned for Nick to follow him outside. "I'll call Amy and see if she's heard anything. Meantime, you backtrack to the warehouse and see if you can find her."

Nick pulled into the warehouse parking lot and saw Tracy's car, noting the flat tire. He pulled alongside, got out and walked around the vehicle, then looked inside. She would have had a bag of some sort with her gear. He saw nothing. The warehouse door was locked, so she probably wasn't in there, but he rang the bell anyway. No answer. Surely, if she had called a cab she would've been at the tournament by now. Maybe he had just missed her.

Nick dialed Shane's number. "Anything yet?"

"Tracy called Amy half an hour ago but hung up before she could answer. She said the guys got there with the desk about ten minutes ago. They told her Tracy was locking up when they left."

"I found her car in the warehouse parking lot with a flat. She wasn't anywhere around. I thought maybe she got a ride, but she would've been there by now."

"Something happened. Maybe someone came along and picked her up because Amy said the phone only rang a couple of times then stopped."

"That's strange. Now, I'm getting a little nervous."

"What do you want to do?"

"You stay there in case she shows up and I'll drive around town and see if I can pick up on anything. If we don't hear from her soon, I'm calling the cops." Still searching for a plausible explanation, he added, "I don't even know where to begin to look for her."

Nick called the cab company and asked if any of the drivers had picked up a fare at the warehouse and he gave him the address. There was a long silence and the dispatcher came back on the line.

"No, it's been slow today, Nick. None of our guys have even been on that end of town."

"Thanks, Joe. I appreciate your help." Nick disconnected the call and took a deep ragged breath. This wasn't good. He felt a weakness deep in his gut, an old form of a bad premonition that had always proved to be right. It had been a long time since he felt it, but he remembered the feeling well.

Tracy sat on the sofa, her fingers tensed in her lap, trying to come up with a plan. No one would find her here. She either had to find a way to let someone know where she was, or convince Garth to take her back into town. If she could get to her cell phone—

"Could I get my purse from the car?"

"No, and you're not going to get anything until you tell me where that necklace is. Is that clear?" The angry retort hardened his features, and his eyes blazed with anger.

"I have to go to the bathroom."

"No."

"Then you can clean up after me because if you don't let me go, I'll relieve myself right here. So far there's nothing to connect me to you, but if I go right here, there will be DNA evidence in this cabin linked to you."

"All right!"

"I need my purse."

"To use the bathroom?"

"There are some personal feminine products in there I need."

Garth glared at her. He was about to make another remark when it dawned on him what she was talking about. "Oh, right. We'll both go to the car and you can get your purse."

"Thank you," she managed to reply through stiff lips. Now, if her luck held he wouldn't think about the phone being in there.

Leaning across the car's seat, her back to Garth, Tracy slipped her hand down into the purse and grabbed the phone. She stashed it in the waistband of her skirt, while her other hand reached for the gym bag.

"Leave that one and just get your purse." Back in the cabin, he took the purse and started to look through it.

"If you don't mind, I don't want you pawing through my personal things." She snatched the purse, but he evidently was satisfied with what he saw because he didn't try to get it back.

"It's down the hall and to the right. Don't even think about climbing out the window, Chapman. It won't work. And in case you decide to scream, it won't do you any good. There's no one for miles around to hear. Besides, I'll be right outside the door."

"I didn't know you were a pervert, too."

"There are a lot of things you don't know about me," his lips twisted in a cynical smile. "Don't push your luck."

So far there was no proof he had Amy. She would see for herself. Although the shop was closed today, someone had to be there to let in the men with the desk. Amy volunteered because she didn't have the "constitution", she said, to watch the kickboxing event.

Tracy pulled out her phone and dialed the shop. She waited through several rings. No answer. There wasn't much time; soon Garth would begin to get suspicious. Punching in another number, she hoped he wouldn't hear her talk. It wouldn't surprise her, though, if he had his ear to the door, listening to make sure she didn't try to escape.

When Nick answered, she whispered one word into the phone: "Help!" There was no more time for conversation since she didn't want to make Garth suspicious, but she didn't disconnect the call, either. Instead, she put the phone on the back of the toilet and lifted both lid and seat to hide it. She hoped it would continue to send out a signal, at least long enough to get help. She was sure Nick, being an ex-cop, would try to get someone to locate her phone right away, if that was at all possible.

"Tracy, where are you? Tracy?" Nick held the phone out and looked at the display. She wasn't answering, but it wasn't because the call had been disconnected. She was definitely in trouble. He did a "u" turn in the middle of the street and headed for the police station. He could call Shane from there and have him come down. Hopefully, they could put a trace on the call. Technology had come a long way since he was on the force.

There seemed to be twenty red lights and he was caught by every one of them. Of course, there was never a police officer around when you needed one. By the time he got to the station he was in a highly agitated state. He burst through the door, startling the desk sergeant and a civilian with whom he was speaking.

"Hey, Nick, what's up? Where's the fire?"

"I need to see Don Sandoval. Quick."

The desk sergeant picked up the phone and dialed a number. He spoke quietly into the phone and glanced up at Nick, then said a few more words before hanging up. "He'll be right here."

Sandoval opened the door and motioned to Nick. "What can I do for you, Nick? The sergeant said you seem pretty upset."

"Something has happened to Tracy Chapman, a friend of mine. I don't know if she's been snatched or if she's had an accident and is terribly injured somewhere. She called a few minutes ago and all I heard was a faint cry for help. She didn't or couldn't disconnect the call, so the connection is still open."

"I'll see what I can do. Give me her carrier and phone number and go get yourself a cup of coffee. We'll take it from here."

"Can I use your phone?"

"Sure, help yourself."

While Sandoval was working with the cell phone company, Nick propped on the edge of a nearby desk and called Shane.

"Tracy called Amy again, but she didn't get to the phone in time. Sorry, Amy was busy with a customer at the back of the store. He had come in when the delivery guys were there. When she checked who had called, it was Tracy's cell phone number."

"She called me, too. She's in trouble and we don't know what kind. All she could manage was a weak cry for help. I headed straight for the police station and we still have a connection with her phone. The cops are trying to locate the origin of the signal." Nick checked his watch. Time was critical. "Where are you?"

"Michael and I are on our way to pick up Amy."

"The boyfriend Michael?"

"He got here just after you left. He came in to support Tracy. It was supposed to be a surprise, but I guess that backfired. We'll see you in a few."

The tensing of Nick's jaw betrayed his displeasure over Michael's arrival. He wasn't sure if it was professional or personal. He certainly didn't know enough about the guy to form a personal opinion of him, but boyfriends tended to create a lot of problems at a time like this. Hell, he had more important issues right now than worrying over a cowboy.

Ten minutes later Michael, Amy and Shane were escorted into the squad room. "What's being done to find Tracy?" Michael demanded. "How close are you to finding her?"

Sandoval shot a cold look at Nick. "The boyfriend, Michael something or other," Nick informed him.

"Michael Harris." Michael extended his hand to Sandoval. He turned to Nick; his mouth twisted wryly. "Nick Greger?" His gaze swept up and down Nick as though sizing up an opponent.

"Yeah."

"Any idea what's happened? Where Tracy is?"

"Sorry, you'll have to talk to the officer here. It's a police matter now." Nick turned and headed for the coffee machine. He dug into his pockets for some change just as Shane dropped some quarters into the machine.

"What was that all about? You two have an axe to grind?"

"I've never met the man before." Nick shrugged and raised the cup of coffee. "Thanks."

Shane studied his friend as he sauntered back into the squad room. If he didn't know better he would think Nick was a little jealous. "Naw," he commented aloud.

"Finish your business?" A shadow of annoyance crossed Garth's face. "Now, I want to know where the necklace is and you better tell the truth. I'm losing my patience with you. I might remind you that your friend's safety is at issue here."

"What happened, Garth? Scandal has never been attached to your name."

"Let's just say I have an overwhelming debt to some very scary people and this necklace will give me a chance for a new start somewhere far away from them." A flicker of apprehension coursed through his body. There wasn't much time. Those goons had little patience and what little they had wasn't being practiced on him.

"Gambling or loans?"

"Quit stalling." Garth raised his hand to strike Tracy and by instinct she blocked the attack with a raised arm. "Oh, that's right, you were on your way to some kind of martial arts thing. Very good, Chapman."

"Don't remind me. I worked very hard for this tournament and I was determined to win. Another reason you will pay dearly for this."

"The last time I checked, I had the upper hand here. What makes you think you'll get the chance?"

"What makes you think I won't? Are you planning on killing me?"

"One last time, where is the necklace?" He ground the question out between his teeth.

"And I told you it's with its rightful owner. You're just a shade too late, Garth. I delivered the necklace a few days ago."

"Then we'll go and get it back."

"Not until you release Amy from wherever she's being held. When I know she's safe. "

He slammed one fist against his other hand. "Damn you, Chapman, you're really trying my patience."

"All you have to do is bring Amy here, or take me to see her so I know she is safe. That shouldn't be too hard to do.

Garth paced the floor, running fingers through his hair. He cursed himself for not having planned better. He had thought if he brought Tracy out here where she couldn't get in touch with anyone to verify Amy's safety, she would talk. He had to figure a way out of the situation he had gotten himself into.

Once Tracy found out he didn't have Amy, there wouldn't be any bargaining power. He would just have to find Amy and bring her out here, too. It shouldn't be too difficult since no one would connect him with Tracy's disappearance, even if they had noticed she was gone. It would be just a matter of checking at both shops. What to do with Tracy though? He couldn't take her into town with him.

"You don't really have her, do you?"

"Of course I have her. My friend picked her up about the same time I got you. I'm just trying to figure something out. I can't just leave you free to wander off. "

"Just call your friend and have him bring her here."

"There's no phone."

Standing, she faced him and cleared her throat, a lethal calmness in her eyes. "You can kill me or try to beat it out of me, and I'd love that challenge believe me, but that's it. You'll find out nothing more until I know Amy is safe."

"All right, all right." Garth turned on his heel and searched the kitchen, opening and slamming doors and drawers, rattling utensils. Finally, he found a length of rope beneath the sink. He pulled a chair from the kitchen table and motioned for Tracy to sit down. Next, he tied her hands behind her and looped the rope through the back of the chair, gave it a tug to make sure she couldn't get loose.

"What are you going to do now?"

"What you requested. I'm going to go get Amy and bring her here."

"You're just going to leave me like this? What if something happens, like a fire, or you have an accident and never come back?"

Garth looked at her intently, and then strode to the door without answering her question. *Just like my mother, always asking questions,* he mused. *Where are you going? When will you get back? Who was that on the phone?* He never had a moment's peace. That would all change once he got his hands on the necklace. If it hadn't taken so long to locate a buyer who had no interest in how he acquired such an item, he would have gotten the necklace and be in South America now, enjoying a life of luxury.

Tracy waited until she heard Garth drive away then started trying to free herself. After struggling with the ropes for a few minutes she gave up on that idea. Fortunately he had left her feet free. *He would never make a successful life of crime either*, she thought sardonically.

She leaned forward and lifted the chair off the floor. When Garth opened and closed the drawers she had heard the rattle of silverware. Perhaps there was a knife in there she could use to cut the rope. Walking bent over was a slow process. Each time she moved the chair, it hit against her legs.

Tracy opened the first drawer by clamping her mouth on it's round knob and backing up. No silverware. She opened two more drawers before she found the right one. But when she turned her back to it and tried to get the knife, the chair got in the way. If she pulled the drawer all the way out, the contents would be spilled on the floor and perhaps she would have a better chance of getting one.

Visualizing the step-by-step procedure needed to get the knife off the floor and into her hands to cut the rope, Tracy realized this wouldn't work. She sat back down on the chair, frustration clouding her thoughts. She forced herself to calm down. The minutes ticked away. How long did she have before Garth returned? Suddenly, she remembered her cell phone. Now she had to get down the hall to the bathroom and retrieve her phone.

Her phone was on the commode in front of the tank. She knew if Garth had to use the facility he wouldn't find the phone behind the raised seat. Using her feet to lower the lid and the seat, she swept the phone off the toilet into the wastebasket beside it to cushion the fall. She had to keep the phone in tact. Next, with her feet, she tipped over the wastebasket and carefully scooped the phone out onto the floor.

Then she leaned as far forward as she could and knocked the chair over, squeezing her knees between the chair and floor. When Tracy put her ear down on the phone she found that the connection had been broken. If this was a dropped call she was going to change her provider when this was over!

After several attempts to dial with her tongue, she realized she had to get something stronger, something that would depress the buttons. Struggling, she got to her feet again and went back to the living room and knocked her purse to the floor. She caught the bottom between her teeth and shook the contents onto the floor. There! A pen rolled out. Just what she needed.

Hobbling back to the bathroom with the pen between her teeth, she knelt down and punched in 911.

"911. What is your emergency?"

"This is Tracy Chapman. I'm being held hostage and my captor will be returning soon. I need someone to get here as quickly as possible."

"Where are you, Miss Chapman?"

"In a cabin off the main road north of Monet Cove. There is a long dirt driveway leading up to it."

"How is it marked?"

"I— there was nothing." Tracy tried to recall all she could about the turnoff. Nothing unusual came to mind. Wait! The gate had a faded blue sign. Age had obliterated its letters. She relayed the information to the operator adding, "The man who abducted me is Garth Anderson. I'm not sure if he is the owner of this place."

"Stay with me, Miss Chapman. We'll get help to you." There was silence and then, "There's someone that wants to talk to you. I'll patch you through."

"Tracy? Are you all right?" Nick's frantic voice came on the line.

"So far so good. Nick, he has Amy. He just went to get her."

"Amy's here with us."

"That rotten liar. He knew I wouldn't try anything until I knew she was safe. Just you wait."

"They have found the location of the cabin. Hang in there. We'll see you soon."

Michael and Nick went with Officer Henry to pick up Tracy, while Amy and Shane waited at the police station. Michael was the first one out of the car. He burst into the cabin just as Tracy hobbled up the hall. She was almost afraid to look up in case it was Garth who came through the front door. When she finally looked up and saw Michael, she gulped hard, hot tears slipping down her face.

"I have never been so glad to see anybody in my whole life," she cried.

Michael searched through the utensils scattered on the floor and found a knife. He cut the ropes, then massaged Tracy's hands and arms. She placed her hands on her hips and bent backwards, arching her back. It was good to stand up straight for a change. Michael took her in his arms and held her, releasing her only long enough to look at her, to reassure himself she was really safe.

Nick hung back, watching the scene as casually as he could manage. Now that he saw she was safe, he could relax and hopefully, this brought and end to all the bad players. He turned and walked back toward the police cruiser.

"Nick, hold up." Tracy released Michael and hurried toward the investigator. She wrapped her arms around him and buried her face in his shoulder. "Thank you, my dear friend." She spoke in a suffocated whisper, clinging tightly to him.

"I'm glad you're safe. Now I can get on with my life. I did have a life before all this, you know." His voice broke with huskiness, revealing the depths of his concern.

Tracy was sitting at a desk in the squad room when they brought Garth in. He looked at her with a mocking expression that sent her temper soaring. She lunged, kicking him in the solar plexus. Garth went down on his knees, gasping for breath.

Nick and officer Henry grabbed Tracy on either side. "It's okay, guys. I'm not going to kill him, as wonderful as the idea may be. I just wanted him to suffer for a few minutes and feel terror while he tries to get his breath back.

"Let's get out of here," Michael suggested. "I want to take you home."

"Yours or mine?" There was a trace of laughter in her voice.

"You mean I have a choice this time?"

"We'll see."

* * * * * * * * *

Next week, Tracy was leaving to visit Michael and try to restore some order to her life. Before he left for North Dakota, they had made love, but she had been unable to give herself completely to him. She pondered the problem. Hopefully, when she was on the ranch she would be able to concentrate just on Michael, give herself wholly to him without any distractions. For now she sat on the rock outcropping and watched the moving sea while she tried to gain some inner peace. Could she? There was still a family to be found and she knew the police were doing everything they could. It was a long slow process.

Two weeks had passed since "Jane Doe" died. Her description and the events surrounding her death saturated the television news, but as yet no one had come forth to claim her. Surely someone out there knows and misses this young girl. Where are they and why haven't they come forward? If her family couldn't be found, what would become of Alicia?

Epilogue

Tracy clutched the small round stone as she approached the gate to the Mount Sinai Cemetery. She had carried it all the way from California to bring a token from the state in which Samuel had made his home for the past eighteen years. When Sarah had told her that flowers on Samuel's grave would be all right, but that the Jewish people placed a stone on a grave to show they had been there to pay tribute, she selected the perfect one from her yard.

The funeral had been held shortly after his body arrived and since Tracy had been imprisoned by Garth, she was unable to attend. This pilgrimage was so important to her. It was a time to bid Samuel a personal goodbye.

Two gates, supported by a white pillar on each side, marked the entrance, while a sign proclaiming the name arched above. The gates were locked with a chain but there was a space on one side that allowed a person to walk through. Tall cedar trees encircled the graveyard while a circular driveway cut a path through the green carpet of grass. A lone bird's song competed with the sound of the breeze that whispered through the trees.

"What a lovely place! So private and serene," she said aloud. Sarah had drawn her a map showing where Samuel had been laid to rest. Tracy walked around the cemetery until she found it and knelt down. She bowed her head and had a moment of silence before placing the stone on the grave.

Tracy raised her head and a tear slipped down her cheek. She had been on an incredible journey with Samuel through his journal, and it was with a deep sadness that she told him farewell. He was on a journey now that no one could share.

The End

Sandra Farris makes her home in Tucson, Arizona. When she isn't writing she enjoys hiking, gardening and most things that take place outside. Sandra retired from a government job to devote her time to writing. She is currently working on her fifth and sixth books.

Dan Farris lives in Hastings, Nebraska, where he runs a beef business. He writes in his spare time and is currently working on a music album and another book.

CPSIA information can be obtained at www.ICGtesting.com
Printed in the USA
BVOW02*1953090216

436130BV00001B/2/P

9 781440 160509